Mel Foster and the Demon Butler

For Ingrid Hanson

And in loving memory of Richard Hanson, photographer

'It has long been an axiom of mine
that the little things are infinitely
the most important.'

– *Sherlock Holmes*

Contents

Chapter One
The Thing in the Ice

The director of the orphanage had predicted that Mel would come to a bad end. Looking at the sea of ice, Mel decided this was probably it. He was about to meet a bad end at a very bad end of the world, a place the sailors called the North Pole, or as near as a ship could get.

The *Albatross* had been stuck since midnight and the sea at the stern had solidified. There was ice everywhere – and not a crack or a chink through which they could escape. The seamen said it was now a waiting game: would the ship's sides cave in under the pressure or would they all die of cold and hunger first?

'A third choice, please,' Mel muttered as he bent over his sail-mending, but no one took any notice of the cabin boy. Usually a sunny-natured person, gifted in making mischief and breaking rules, the prospect of imminent death was dampening even Mel's high spirits. He sat back against the ship's lifeboat on the main deck, huddled in the canvas he was sewing, trying to think of a bright side to the situation.

Nope. There wasn't one.

He blew on the tips of his fingers, nimbly ducking the cuffs of passing crewmen.

'Your orders, Captain Mariner?' called Able Seaman Ishmael. The sailor was leaning over the side, thumping the ice with a pole to gauge the thickness. Ishmael had a shaven head tattooed with a map of the world which he'd had done in Singapore. Unfortunately, the ink had been substandard and become a puddle of blue like a bruise.

No finding your way home from that noggin, thought Mel.

The captain appeared on the balcony of the bridge, ten feet above the main deck. The iron plating was treacherous and his peg leg slipped on the ice. He flung out an arm and gripped the railing with his hook, producing a teeth-aching screech of metal on metal. A veteran of a hundred voyages, his single brown eye burned with fiery defiance against the terrible odds they faced. Captain Mariner had surrendered so many bits of his body to nature – to storms, sharks and scurvy – that he had no intention of giving up any of his remaining limbs to frost.

'Take a party of men over the side, Mr Ishmael. We'll

cut our way free, damn my eye if we don't.'

Mr Wallace, the scientific explorer who had commissioned this voyage to the north, popped up at the captain's side like a jack-in-the-box. To Mel, his shiny pink face looked like a partially sucked boiled sweet spat out on the pavement. From the scientist's eager expression, it was clear that he had no notion of the danger they were in.

'But we can't retreat, captain!' exclaimed Mr Wallace, his voice a squeak of excitement. 'We're so close!'

'Close to our deaths, sir.' The hook now pressed against the scientist's chest, snagging on an ivory button. 'We have proved beyond doubt that you cannot sail to the Pole even at the height of summer. If you persist in your intention of planting the British flag on that spot, your only recourse is to go on by foot. I believe it is that way.' The captain swept his hook to the featureless north. 'Good luck to you.'

Mr Wallace smoothed down the ruffled fur of his coat. 'But . . . but I have no sledge – no dogs!'

'Then it seems this expedition is at an end. We turn back – if we can.'

The captain clumped away, leaving the scientist facing a prospect of ruined ambitions. He gave a little whimper, like a kicked puppy.

Mel shook his head in disgust. Mr Wallace was a complete waste of cargo space!

'You heard the captain, lads. Look lively.' Ishmael

gathered a party of the stoutest men in the crew and they lowered the boat over the side of the vessel. The *Albatross* was a rusty black steamer with a single smokestack and two masts to assist the engines. The warmth from the boilers kept the sea around the stern from freezing, but a few feet further off the cold was winning.

'Boy, come keep the brazier alight.' Ishmael had put a small stove on board the ship's boat to warm the ice-smashing party. He was one of the kinder men on the crew. The other seamen had no patience with the succession of cabin boys they called Lady B's Orphans. They enjoyed plaguing the youngsters. Mel had been told that none of his predecessors had survived more than six months, and Mel had already managed five.

Perhaps he wouldn't make the full six after all?

Glad to have something to do other than wait for death, Mel slid down the rope to join the men. Overhead, a bow of green light writhed snakelike across the dark blue expanse, twisting from east to west. Some of the more superstitious men crossed themselves.

''Tis only the Northern Lights,' scoffed Ishmael. As an American from Nantucket, land of the free and home of reason, he had no patience with Old World beliefs that said the glow marked the passage of a demon to Earth.

Pulling his woollen cap over his ears, Mel sketched a secret little cross over his heart. Better safe than sorry.

A hungry wind prowled the snowy wastes. At the edge of the sea ice, four men clambered out, ropes tied round their middles. The remainder of the party stayed in the boat, primed to reel their fellows in quickly. No one could survive more than a second or two in that water. The advance team called out that the ice was thick enough to support their weight, so the rest were given the order to follow.

Ishmael passed out the hatchets, pickaxes and poles. The seamen began hacking at the ice on two sides. The plan was to carve notches like a tram track, break up the ice in between and so clear a space for the hull to plough through. Further on, a second party of men lit fires in hopes that the ice would melt and be easier to remove. Mel poked the brazier in the ship's boat. It didn't take a genius to know that this method of retreat would be too slow, like a snail trying to ascend Mount Everest. He cupped his hands, blowing on the bluish tips of his fingers. His knitted gloves had worn away at the ends and he was in constant danger of frostbite. He rubbed his palms together, then tucked his hands under his armpits and huddled by the hot metal side of his stove. At least for now he was warm; it could be worse. He whistled a snatch of a favourite song to keep his spirits up.

After several hours of chipping and hauling ice, the ship had retreated about a hundred yards from where she had come to a halt that morning. The men were now hauling a huge block out of the water, much thicker than the sheets they had previously removed. From his vantage point, looking at it sideways, Mel caught a glimpse of a black streak trapped inside the ice. If he had to place a bet on what it was, he would plump for a dead seal or fish. Preserved in ice, it might serve to feed the crew and keep starvation at bay a few more days.

'Mr Ishmael.' Mel stood up and waved at the able seaman. 'I think there's something inside that piece.'

With colourful curses, the men heaved the block on to the ice floe. Once out of the water the slab proved much easier to move, as they could slide it. Ishmael ordered the men to spin the block so he could see what they had caught.

He scratched his bald head somewhere near Australia. 'The boy's right. Here: light this.' He passed Mel a pole with a pitch-covered rag at the end.

Dipping the tip in the brazier, Mel then clambered out of the boat to hand it back. Ishmael held the flames against the place where the black streak was nearest the surface. In the rippling heat of the fire, the ice began to melt. When he judged that he had done enough, he handed the torch to Mel and knelt down by the side of the block. Taking off a glove, he broke off the last film of ice and touched the thing.

'By the great whale . . . it can't be!' He whipped his hand away as if he had been burned.

Mel crouched beside him. 'Is that . . .' he swallowed,

feeling sick, 'is that *human* hair?'

'Mr Ishmael, why have you stopped work?' called the captain from the stern of the *Albatross*.

'We've found something, sir.' Ishmael hurriedly put his glove back on. 'A body in the ice.'

A few feet away from the captain, Mr Wallace craned his head over the side. 'A body, you say? Oh, that is wonderful!'

Not for the poor victim, thought Mel sourly.

'I've heard of finding mammoths in the ice, but never a human. It could be the missing link to prove that humans came from apes, as Mr Darwin claims. Bring it on board and let me examine it!'

Mel added 'wildly optimistic' to the other things he knew about the scientist.

Captain Mariner scowled at Wallace. 'Whose ship is this, sir?'

'Um, yours?' replied the scientist, just intelligent enough to give the right answer.

'I give the orders here. We've no time for idle scientific curiosity.'

Mr Wallace looked dismayed for a second but then searched for a persuasive argument. 'Captain, think how much credit this discovery will bring. We live in an age of marvels and the great monster hunt is on. Strange discoveries are dug up daily all over the Empire: bones of creatures as big as dragons – mummies and shrunken heads – fortunes built, reputations made. You want to be part of that, don't you?'

The bristling black brow over the captain's remaining eye shot up. 'Fortunes?'

'Yes, yes. The Queen is bound to pay well to see this wonder. The more unusual, the more she will give. Think how much a half-ape, half-human will bring!'

'If it is an ape-man. It is more likely to be an unfortunate sailor who went over the side from a whaler.'

'Then let's bring it aboard and examine it more closely.'

Captain Mariner rubbed the scarred space where his left eye had once been. 'Men, bring that thing aboard.'

'But sir, it weighs close to a ton!' objected Ishmael. 'Shouldn't we melt the ice from it first?'

'It mustn't be completely unfrozen or it will rot away before we can reach London.' Deciding to join the party on the ice, Mr Wallace was now struggling with the ropes to climb over the side. The captain gestured to a sailor to assist him. As much as the crew despised their passenger, no one wished to dump the man who paid their wages into the Arctic Ocean. That would put an end to any hope of a bonus.

The captain was already losing interest in the find, content that it would keep Mr Wallace out of his way. 'Mr Ishmael, melt as much of the block as you deem necessary but, for the love of Neptune, send the men back to work smashing a course through this cursed ice. Put the boy on the task – he can be spared.'

'Aye aye, captain.' Ishmael ordered two sailors to lift the brazier out of the boat and place it on a wooden pallet so Mel could move it slowly around the block. He handed Mel a scraper and chisel. 'You understand what you have to do?'

'Aye, Mr Ishmael.'

'Carry on then.'

Mel picked up his tools and hacked at a corner, humming to himself.

Mr Wallace staggered across the ice to where Mel was working.

'No, no, this will not do.' He gestured to the black hair straggling out of the hole Ishmael had made.

'Sir?' Mel tried to sound polite.

'We can't have the ape-man exposed like that. You need to make sure that part goes under ice again.'

Mel scratched his nose. How was he to both melt and freeze the body? Mr Wallace had no idea how difficult his task was already in the sub-zero temperatures.

It's a good job, Mel thought, *that I'm not easily spooked*. Life in the orphanage had cured Mel of that: he'd often had to help the undertaker. Among the coffins and wood shavings he had learned then that bodies were just bodies; rich and poor, young and old, everyone was the same in death. 'I'll do my best, sir.'

The chill penetrating his thick fur coat, sheepskin gloves and fleece-lined boots, Mr Wallace slipped his way back to the ship, leaving the cabin boy, dressed only in woollens and ragged hand-me-down trousers, to finish the job.

Mel sighed and moved the brazier. He chipped away at the ice, deciding he would deal with the removal before he attempted to restore a covering to the head. *Chip-chip*. The block whittled away piece by piece. Wind licked his cheeks. In the long daylight of the northern summer, the fragments of ice glinted. They brought to mind the diamond necklace he had once seen around a noblewoman's neck, a rare flash of beauty in his life. Lady Bracknell had worn the gems to visit the poor unfortunates at Mr Squeers's Orphanage and wrongly thought the attention of the children had been for her. To a soul, they had been calculating how many pies just one of those jewels would purchase. Lady Bracknell had passed down the line of orphans and finally reached Mel, one of the oldest inmates.

'And you are?' she had demanded, her gold spectacles held to her eyes as she inspected him like an insect pinned to a card.

'Melchizedek John Foster, m'lady.'

'Ha ha ha!' Her laugh had caught everyone by surprise, matching their shock when Mel had released a box of frogs in the middle of the Sunday sermon. 'What an extraordinarily large name for so small a person.'

'It was chosen by Dr Foster, the gentleman who found the boy while on a visit to Gloucester. The doctor is a patron of this establishment,' explained Mr Squeers quickly, as if he had to apologize for the selection of one so grand. He pointed to the smiling portrait of Dr Foster that presided over the dining room, transferring the blame to Mel's sponsor.

'Boy, what do you think of your name?' asked the lady. She smelt faintly of lavender water and smoke. Iron-grey hair swirled high on her head like a guardsman's helmet.

'I think I might grow into it, given time,' Mel said cautiously. He was proud of his name – he had found it in the Bible, which gave it the ultimate stamp of approval.

'Indeed, you might. Or you might not.' She dug in her handbag and pulled out a folded banknote. 'This boy, Mr Squeers: this is the one I will send to join the merchant navy.' She handed him the money. Her cold smile was not reassuring.

With that announcement, Mel's future had been decided.

'And now I'm chipping ice off a corpse,' Mel muttered to himself. 'Look how far I've come.' Wiping away the fragments, he stepped back to take a better look. The ice distorted its contents, but he guessed the creature was about seven feet long with masses of dark hair. Oddly, it seemed to be wearing a white dress. It then occurred to him that it could be a shroud. Sailors were buried at sea sewn up in sailcloth, last stitch through the nose to check they were really dead. The ocean had begun to unwrap this one. The chances of it being an ape-man were fast disappearing, royal favour and scientific prizes vanishing like steam from the smokestack. Mr Wallace was not going to be pleased.

Peeking over his shoulder to check no one was watching, Mel stuck his fingers into the hole Ishmael had made. The hair was silky soft. The temptation to go further was akin to picking at a scab, wrong but impossible to resist. He wriggled his fingers deeper so he could touch the scalp. Strange: it felt warmer than his own skin. A little flick of static cracked between his fingertip and the thing's head.

'How are you getting on, boy?' called Ishmael.

Mel snatched back his hand. 'Very good, sir. Almost done, I think.'

'Then let's get it aboard. Ewan, Matthews: help Mel get that thing on to the ship.'

Sliding two ropes around the coffin-shaped ice block, the sailors used the loading tackle to lift the corpse up to the deck. The job passed with relative ease now that Mel had removed most of the ice.

'Where do ye want this stowed, captain?' asked Ewan. A burly Scotsman, Ewan had frost on his bristling red beard and brows.

'In the hold,' said the captain. 'Mr Wallace can play with it there.' He scowled at the men on the ground. 'Mr Ishmael, bore holes in the sea ice and see how thick it is. I am minded to ram a passage.'

Mel decided to follow the thing. Having been on the ice for most of the day he thought he deserved a chance to warm up. He clambered down the ladders to the deepest of the storage compartments, cheeks tingling in the relative warmth of the interior.

'*Things are seldom what they seem*,' he sang under his breath, picking up a popular tune that had been doing the rounds of the London glee clubs before he left on this voyage. '*All that glitters is not gold*.' He looked forward to the moment of the scientist's comeuppance.

When he got to the hold he found Mr Wallace instructing the sailors to pack the slab with straw on a narrow shelf. Pleased to be rid of it, Ewan banged the block into the steel side of the ship. The resulting boom sounded ominous.

'Careful now: we mustn't spoil it!' squawked Wallace.

'What do ye think tha' is, sir?' asked Ewan as he held a lantern over the face. Hair obscured the blurred features.

'Ugly looking bug, ain't he, guv?' smirked Matthews, a thin cockney with no more bulk than a bundle of sticks.

'It is not a bug.' Wallace frowned at the sailors. 'It is the missing link.' He patted the ice, his signet ring rapping on the surface. 'This discovery will make us famous.'

The ice cracked. Like an egg hatching, the split travelled all the way through the block and a large fragment sheared off.

'Quick, do something, men!' Mr Wallace tried to push the ice back together but he didn't have enough hands to accomplish the task. 'I told the captain it was too warm down here! Oh, dodo droppings! It's coming apart.'

It was far too late to stop the ice falling away: half the body was exposed, one arm dangling, blackened nails touching the floor.

'Tha' isna ape-man,' said Ewan.

'No sailor neither,' added Matthews with ghastly relish.

'It's a girl,' said Mel, creeping a little closer.

'No, that's not a human!' Mr Wallace peered at the arm with a magnifying glass. 'Gentlemen, we have found ourselves a genuine monster!'

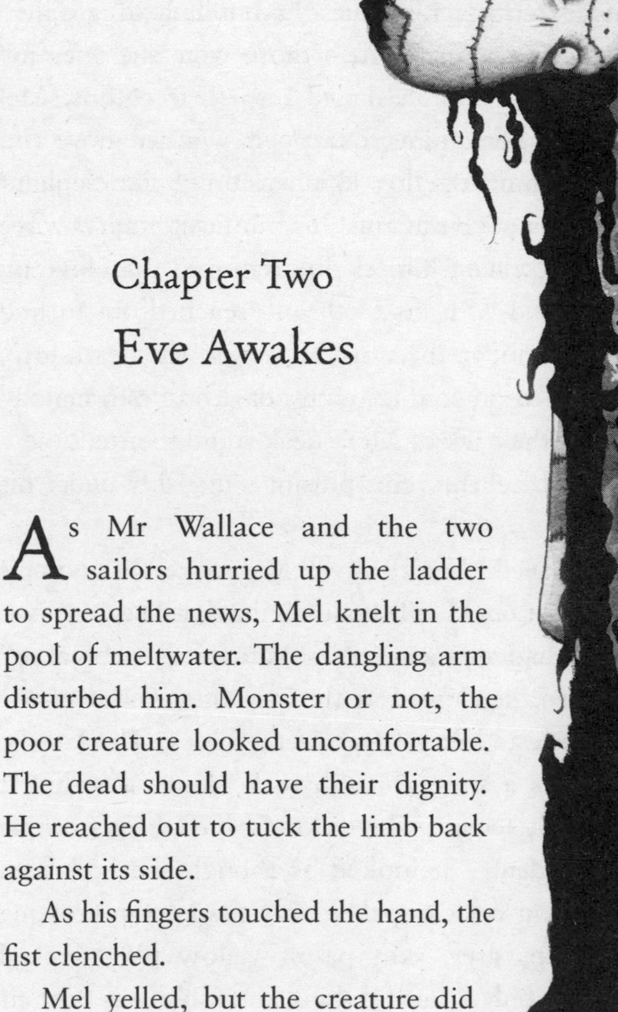

Chapter Two
Eve Awakes

As Mr Wallace and the two sailors hurried up the ladder to spread the news, Mel knelt in the pool of meltwater. The dangling arm disturbed him. Monster or not, the poor creature looked uncomfortable. The dead should have their dignity. He reached out to tuck the limb back against its side.

As his fingers touched the hand, the fist clenched.

Mel yelled, but the creature did not move again.

'It's just a reflex,' he told himself, heart still pounding with shock. Sometimes in the orphanage mortuary, bodies had twitched, groaned or even sat up after death – those were the ones the funeral director double-nailed into their coffins. Mel tugged but his fingers were trapped, woollen glove and all. The parchment-yellow skin was tough like elephant hide and did not give against his frantic attempts to free his fingers. Steeling himself, he removed the glove on his other hand with his teeth and reached out to find a pressure point in the wrist to release the death grip. Static prickled on contact with not-dead flesh, making the hair on the back of Mel's neck stand to attention.

He could feel the veins pulsing sluggishly under his fingers.

'Triton's teeth! You're alive!' Mel rocked back on his heels. How it could still be living having been encased in ice, he had no idea. 'Air! You need to breathe!' One-handed, he clawed at the ice remaining over the half of the head not yet free of the block. The face he revealed was a strange patchwork of features, but it was definitely female. The girl must have been in some serious accident – it looked as though she had been clumsily sewn back together, scar tissue criss-crossing her face, lips grey, skin palest yellow like plucked poultry. The only beautiful thing about her was the hair that rippled and cascaded to the floor, jet black.

Once her face was clear of ice, Mel set about reviving her. He tapped her cheeks and shouted in her ear. No response. Was he imagining her heartbeat? Perhaps she really was dead and the pulse was a phantom? He grappled for her wrist again. No: it was definitely there.

'Please wake up!' Mel had a very bad feeling about what the sailors would do when they realized their corpse was alive. The majority were superstitious and did not respond well to surprises. Come to think of it, he wasn't sure that he was reacting at all well himself. He felt plain terrified, stomach doing horrible octopus flips and squirms. 'You've got to wake up and let go!' He rubbed desperately at her arm. 'Please, miss, open your eyes.'

The lids fluttered. Slowly, in the feeble light of the lanterns suspended from the ceiling, the lashes parted and eyes blinked, trying to focus. One iris was brown, the other dark blue, the whites watery and yellowed. They swivelled in their sockets to come to rest on Mel's face. Lips pressed together, then opened to reveal strong white teeth.

'Gaargh!' The noise was a throaty gasp. The grip on his hand tightened, threatening to crush bones.

'Please don't hurt me!' Mel now reconsidered the wisdom of waking her by himself. He always suspected that he was a foolhardy idiot. This was proof.

'Gaargh!'

The cry chilled him to the bones; it sounded both threat and plea. He struggled to think what it might mean. The girl had been trapped in ice for heaven knew how long: what could she need?

'Water?' Mel picked up a shard of melting ice and rubbed it along her cracked lips. He was rewarded when she sucked greedily at the piece.

Hang on a minute, pea-brain, he thought, *sea ice would be too salty*. He reached for the flask of rum-and-water that he carried clipped to his belt. He dribbled a few drops into her mouth. The hit of the rum at the back of the throat caused the girl to shiver violently. The last pieces of ice cracked and she rolled on to her side, still holding on to Mel like an anchor.

'M . . . mm,' she mumbled.

'More?' guessed Mel, holding out the flask. He was trembling all over; it was only her grip on his hand that kept him from sinking to the floor like a beached jellyfish.

With painful slowness, the girl swung her legs over the side of the shelf and stood up, ice falling from her in chunks. *Neptune's beard!* Mel's guess had not been far off: she was at least seven feet tall. She pushed the flask away.

'*Non, je voudrais dire "merci"*,' she said haltingly, each word hacked out of her throat as her voice box returned to working order.

Mel then realized his proverbial goose was cooked. Not only had he revived a giant girl without waiting for the captain's command, but, worse than that, she'd turned out to be French.

*

'You found a monster, you say?' Captain Mariner's strident voicc signalled his approach from the deck above.

'Yes, sir, an extraordinary discovery for British science. There have been hints that monsters existed among us – theories that folklore held more fact than fiction – but we'll be the first to confirm it with a well-preserved specimen! The name of this voyage will rival that of Darwin's *Beagle* in the history books, you mark my words.' Mr Wallace sounded as if he had already written the headline for the newspapers.

'Only if we manage to return,' said the captain sourly. 'Right, where is it?' The handle of the lantern squeaked as he thrust it into the dark space of the shelf. 'There's nothing there, man! It's melted away.'

'Impossible!'

Backed up against the hull in the shadows, Mel could feel the giantess trembling behind him. It wasn't a scared tremble, more a prepared-to-attack quiver. She still held his hand and he really preferred not to be around for the confrontation between monster and sailors.

'Search the ship,' ordered the captain. 'See if the thing has been moved.'

Ewan cleared his throat and pointed. 'Ah, captain, sir.'

The four men in the hold – the captain, Wallace, Ewan and Matthews – swivelled to face Mel and the giantess.

'Neptune's trident, what is that?' asked Captain Mariner, his eye bulging from its socket.

'She's got the laddie.' Ewan's gaze darted to the ladder exit. 'Do ye think she intends to eat him?'

That was a new and unwelcome notion. Mel tried to prise her fingers off his hand but she held firm. It was an uncomfortable position; she might be alive but she was very cold and damp. Wet was seeping through the back of Mel's clothes where they were touching and now he also had to consider whether he was on the menu for dinner.

Wallace found some courage from a forgotten store of finer emotions. He took a step forward. 'Unhand the boy, monster.'

The giantess growled.

'Sh . . . she's French,' Mel said hoarsely.

That news stumped the men.

'Mr Wallace, you're an educated sort of chap: speak to it,' ordered the captain.

'Um, *lettez go le petit boy*,' tried Wallace.

'You don't speak French, do you, Wallace?' Captain Mariner picked up the chisel Mel had used to chip away the ice.

'No, captain,' admitted the scientist. 'I speak a bit of Latin though.'

'Fat lot of good that is,' muttered Matthews.

The giantess had had enough. She picked Mel up and took a step forward, carrying him like a parcel. 'I speak English. I go now. Goodbye.'

The captain blocked her path to the ladder, waving

the chisel in front of him. 'You cannot pass.'

She slapped the chisel from his hand as if it were no more than a toothpick. It flew to stick in the side of a wooden packing case, quivering slightly. 'You wrong. I very strong. I go.' As swift as a mountain goat, she scaled the ladder, Mel clutched under her arm.

I was mistaken, thought Mel frantically, this *is going to be my bad end: as a meal for a giantess.*

The creature emerged on to the deck and blinked in the daylight. The sailors fell back from her in alarm. She was a horrid sight: straggling black hair over yellowish scarred body, mismatched eyes rolling from left to right, a boy stuffed under one arm like a loaf of bread. Mel scrambled to remember the few words of French he had learned during a stopover in Calais.

'*Je ne suis pas une baguette.*' She frowned down at him. '*Mademoiselle. S'il vous plaît.*' His halting French must have amused her for she broke into a ghastly smile. The teeth were pleasant enough; it was the gaps in her cheeks that showed the tendons and muscles at work that terrified Mel.

'I know you are not bread. You are boy.' She gazed at the desolate landscape around the ship. Sailors were throwing bottles and ice blocks at her back but she did not appear to notice. They bounced off with a thud and a smash. 'Where are we?'

'The North Pole.'

She gave a deep sigh; more a groan really, Mel

thought. 'Where is my father?'

Mel gulped. 'You mean there are more of you?'

'Just my father.'

'No mother?'

'There is only us two.' She scanned the horizon, as though expecting to see her father running towards her.

'How is that possible?'

She turned sad blue-brown eyes on him. 'Victor Frankenstein made my father, and my father, he made me.'

Mel was tired of being held sideways, not least because some of the missiles were striking his feet. 'Can you put me down, please, mademoiselle?'

She placed him in front of her, sheltering him from the hail of objects lobbed at her. 'Where did you find me?'

Mel pointed to the ice below. 'Just there.'

'Alone?'

'Yes. Until we came along. We're stuck in the ice too.'

Something wet splashed on top of his head. He looked up to see a huge crystal tear dripping from her chin. The idea that she had ever meant to eat him now seemed ridiculous. She appeared jolly decent for a monster.

'Then he is gone.' She sniffed. 'What year is this, boy?'

'1895, of course.'

She hung her head, hair draping around them both like a curtain. It had the salty, damp odour of old sails.

'Sixty years. I have been in ice sixty years. He would have rescued me if he were alive.'

'You can't have been in there so long. How can you have survived?' Then again: what was she? No ordinary girl could be so strong, so big, so . . . patched together.

She gripped his shoulders, fingers digging in painfully, but Mel didn't think she realized. She threw back her head and roared with grief. '*PAPA*! *Où es-tu*?'

The sound of rifle bolts being pulled back greeted her cry. Mel peered through her hair to find they were surrounded. Ten sailors stood with guns at their shoulders, eyes squinting down the sights.

'Step away from the boy or we will shoot,' said the captain.

Uh-oh. Now this really was the end. If they fired, odds were they would hit him too. He knew for a fact that three of the sailors were terrible shots.

'Monster, did you hear me?' barked the captain.

The giantess hugged Mel closer to her chest but held her head up defiantly. 'I am Eve Frankenstein. I am beautiful. I am loved. No one calls me monster.'

With that, she pushed Mel out of the way of the firing squad and leapt over the side. Mel threw himself flat on the deck. Guns blasted over his head but the bullets passed into thin air.

'Where's she gone?' Captain Mariner rushed to the side, shoving men from his path. Mel slid through the crowd to see. Eve was striding towards the ice-cutting party. On her approach, the men screamed and dropped their tools, running for the sanctuary of the ship. Seizing a pickaxe, Eve smashed it down on the ice, lifting slabs off the water as easily as a cook skinning custard.

'I make way for you,' she shouted. 'I make a path for my friend, Boy. Then you leave me in peace.'

Mel hugged his waist for comfort as well as warmth, feeling sad for her but also hugely grateful that she would do this for him. All he had done was wake her up and offer her something to drink. It didn't take much to become Eve Frankenstein's friend.

Ishmael was the last of the cutting party up the side of the *Albatross*. He joined the captain at the rail. 'What in Moby Dick's name is that?'

The captain scowled, eyebrows drawn together like fighting caterpillars. 'Some kind of fiend or monster. She woke up when the ice melted.'

'Do you think she means to do it, sir? Free us?'

Captain Mariner tapped his hook on the side, the point scratching the paintwork. 'Aye, I think she does.'

'Magnificent monster,' marvelled Mr Wallace, scribbling notes in his pocketbook. She had already made more progress freeing the ship from the ice than the men had managed all day. 'I trust you will not leave her here, despite her words. The Royal Academy of Sciences must see her. With the Queen's permission, they'll want to exhibit her – prove our theories on monsters before a wondering and wealthy public.'

'What'll you do, captain?' asked Ishmael.

'Allow her to do what she wants,' said the captain, a calculating expression on his face. Mel knew that look. It usually meant someone was about to suffer a painful fate.

'And then?' asked Ishmael.

'It wouldn't do to leave an unprotected . . . um . . . female all alone here, now would it?' The captain's hook tapped out a Morse code of malice on the rail. 'I'm sure she'll want to go with her little friend, Boy.'

Mel opened his mouth to object but Ishmael spoke first.

'How can you make her, sir? You've seen how strong she is. No chain or cage could hold her.'

'We don't need a chain, not while we've got him.' Hand shooting out, the captain seized Mel by the ear and dragged him forward. 'Mr Ishmael, lock Master Melchizedek in the brig and put a guard on him. An armed guard. If the monster won't cooperate, order the guard to shoot the boy.'

'You won't kill him, surely, sir?' asked Ishmael uneasily.

'Of course not. He's worth more alive as our ball and chain. Shoot him in the left leg, and if that doesn't convince her, then the right. The child can lose a limb or two and carry on. I should know.' The captain clumped away, whistling a merry tune.

Chapter Three
Something Fishy at the Palace

'Lord Rosebery is here to see you, Your Majesty.' The private secretary to Queen Victoria stood at the door to the royal apartments, bent over at the keyhole as he issued his respectful announcement. Dressed in severest black, elderly Mr Copperfield took the shape of the illustration of the letter 'r' in a child's primer. Behind him a gaggle of the country's most important men stood waiting on Queen Victoria's pleasure.

'We are not receiving.' The Queen's high, cross voice was unmistakable. Something thumped against the door then crashed on the marble tiles, suggesting an ornament had been relocated from the mantelpiece to the floor.

Mr Copperfield turned back to the government

delegation. 'She is not receiving,' he intoned, as if they hadn't heard that plainly themselves.

'What do you mean, man?' asked Lord Rosebery, the prime minister. 'She must see me! I have to tender my resignation. There's a change of government in the offing.'

Mr Copperfield bristled with offended pride. 'Must, sir? May I remind you that this is Her Imperial Majesty you are talking about: Queen-Empress of India and lands of the British Empire.'

Lord Rosebery, a goggle-eyed man with an unfortunate side parting, looked close to planting a facer square on the private secretary's nose. Evidently, the prime minister was not having a good day. Mr Copperfield took a step back. 'Look, Copperfield, you infuriating individual, I lost the vote in Parliament! I have to resign and Her Imperial Majesty is the only one who can accept.'

'Humph.' With great dignity, Mr Copperfield gathered himself for another knock. 'Your Majesty, your prime minister is here. He says it is very important.'

Lord Rosebery joined him at the keyhole. 'Indeed it is, ma'am. Of utmost importance to the country.'

'Go! Away!' Two objects hit the door in rapid succession.

The prime minister sprang back in consternation. He sniffed. 'Good lord, what is that foul odour, Copperfield? I swear that it is coming from the throne room.'

Eighty-year-old Mr Copperfield blushed. The Queen's chambers were his responsibility and he knew he was failing. 'Her Majesty refuses to allow staff to enter. She ordered a mermaid last week and I fear it is spoiled.'

'A mermaid! What madness is this?'

'Sssh!' Mr Copperfield hopped on the spot. 'Please do not speak that word here.'

'Explain yourself, man!'

Mr Copperfield beckoned the prime minister to stand back from the door – a request with which Lord Rosebery happily complied as the smell was quite disgusting. 'You recollect that the Queen has declared a reward for anyone who proves that monsters exist, as some of her scientists claim?'

'Naturally. We have ransacked the Empire for her entertainment: pygmies and porcupines, snake charmers and salamanders – all have been paraded before her, but she was not amused. Not monstrous enough, apparently.' Lord Rosebery crossed his arms. 'But mermaids and monsters are a myth for a very good reason: they don't exist.'

Mr Copperfield was no longer so sure about that, after what he had seen recently. 'But Her Majesty was most insistent.' Mr Copperfield shivered, remembering the tantrum. 'So her new butler, Mr Albert Burlington, found one at short notice.' Mr Copperfield dropped his voice a peg lower so the government had to crowd round him to hear. 'I fear it was a stitch-up job.'

'A fraud?' asked the minister for the Board of Trade.

'I mean literally a stitch-up: dolphin tail and comely girl. Mr Burlington had a pool built in the throne room for the purpose. The young person left after entertaining Her Majesty with her hair-combing-and-singing-on-a-rock routine. She is now back in the chorus at the Savoy theatre. The tail remains.'

'And the Queen has not noticed?' Lord Rosebery glanced at his fellow ministers. 'This is not good news. Who is with her now?'

'Just Mr Burlington.' Mr Copperfield's mouth pursed. 'And he has claimed the reward.'

'Summon him.'

'But, sir . . .' Mr Copperfield shook in his boots.

But the prime minister had decided that enough was enough. For a few more hours, until the Queen accepted his resignation, Lord Rosebery could at least claim the privilege of his station. 'Am I not the prime minister? Call him.'

Clearing his throat, the private secretary went to the door. 'Mr Burlington, if you would be so good to give us a moment of your time?'

Silence.

'Please, Mr Burlington, we would be much obliged.'

The door cracked open. Mr Copperfield caught a glimpse of a darkened room lit only by candles and the glint of a diamond crown over a ghostly face before the butler slid through the gap and shut the door smartly behind him.

'Mr Burlington, may I present the prime minister,' said Mr Copperfield.

That was all wrong – and Mr Copperfield knew it. A humble butler should be presented to a lord, not the other way round, but he couldn't help himself. Mr Burlington always sent his knowledge of etiquette running for cover.

'Things are clearly going to the dogs at the Palace,' muttered Lord Rosebery. He drew himself up to his full height to issue a reprimand, only to have it die on his lips. His eyes bulged to alarming proportions as he took in Mr Albert Burlington. The butler towered before him: black frock coat, blood-red waistcoat, shiny shoes, bone-white gloves, but no shirt. No one could get past the butler's muscular chest, smooth of hair. It had a caramel sheen like toffee.

'Lord Rosebery,' said Mr Burlington, his voice a near whisper. 'Charmed, I'm sure.' The butler had a handsome face with angled jaw, flowing auburn locks and long sideburns; but the next most disconcerting thing about him after his glaring lack of shirt were his eyes. They were a bright green but on occasion they glinted fiery red in their depths. Mr Copperfield could not help but feel that they were not seeing the real man, but only what the butler wished them to perceive.

Peer of the realm, man of secure inherited wealth, leader of the country though he was, Lord Rosebery trembled. 'Burlington.' He gave the man a sharp nod, attempting to mask his unease.

'I am afraid Her Majesty is not receiving. She has made her wishes quite plain.'

Lord Rosebery screwed up his courage to the sticking place. 'But the matter cannot be delayed. I have to resign, and if she does not accept my resignation then the country – nay, the whole Empire – will be in limbo.'

The butler merely waited.

'We will be without a government.'

No response, but the air thickened with a dark intangible threat.

Sweat trickled down Lord Rosebery's brow. 'She's not receiving today, you say?'

Burlington arched a brow.

'Maybe tomorrow then?' Lord Rosebery's voice rose in a squeak, something it had not done since he was fourteen.

'Perhaps.'

'You will impress upon her that this matter cannot wait. I am a lame duck now I have lost the vote. The country is effectively without a prime minister until she appoints another in my place.'

'Lame duck,' repeated Burlington. He licked his lips, revealing a surprisingly blackened tongue.

'Yes . . . er . . . very good. Carry on then. As you were.'

Without acknowledging Lord Rosebery's attempt to dismiss him, Burlington remained standing before the doors of the throne room.

'I'll . . . er . . . return to Number Ten, then. Pack my bags.' Lord Rosebery took a few wary steps back, the coat-tails of his ministers already whisking around the corner behind him. 'Good day.' He fled, leaving Mr Copperfield to face Burlington alone.

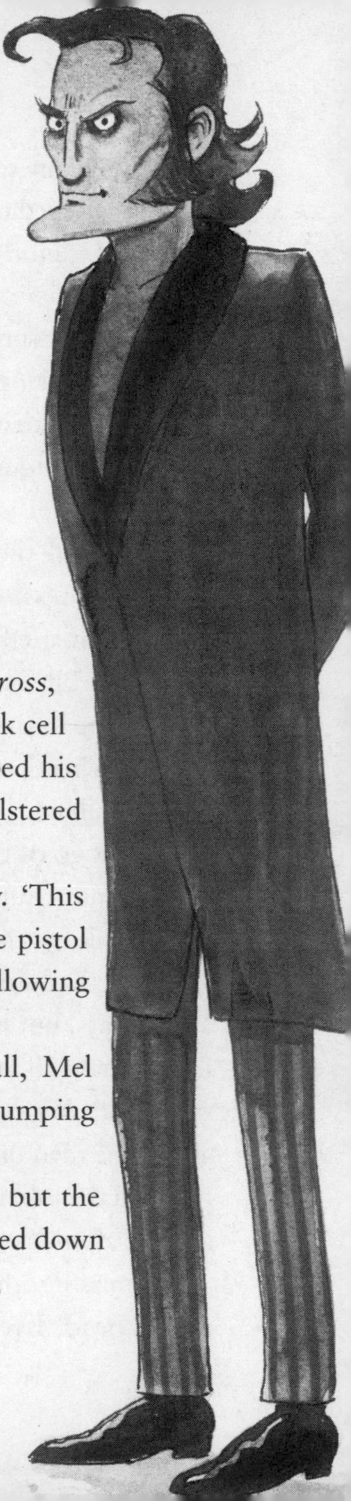

Chapter Four
Spare Parts

Deep in the bowels of the *Albatross*, Ewan stood on guard in the dank cell where he had secured Mel. He combed his fingers through his red beard and unholstered his weapon.

'I'm sorry, laddie,' he said gruffly. 'This isna personal, ye ken.' He cocked the pistol and aimed at Mel's left foot. 'Just following the captain's orders.'

Chained at the ankles to the wall, Mel could not escape. 'Eve!' he yelled, thumping on the hull. 'Help me! *Aidez-moi!*'

The gun went off. Mel screeched, but the expected pain did not follow. He looked down at his feet. Both were still intact.

Ewan grinned. 'Missed. Had ye fooled, though!'

Mel clutched his chest. 'That wasn't funny, Mr Ewan!'

'No, I dinna suppose it was.' Ewan's expression soured. 'I was told to convince the monster that we're serious. Next time the bullet will be on target.'

'Boy? Boy? Are you hurt?' Eve slid down the ladder and landed with a *thunk* that knocked a dent in the floor. She glared through the prison bars at the occupants of the cell. 'I kill you if you hurt him, sailor!' Her fists curled round the iron, and the bars began to buckle under the pressure.

Ewan hurriedly cocked the pistol again. 'Stop that, hell fiend! I'll shoot him if ye try to come in here – and it willna be in the foot this time.' He pointed the gun at Mel's forehead, muzzle wavering in his fear.

Mel gulped.

Eve let go of the bars. 'Boy?'

'I'm not hurt.' Mel slumped against the wall, exhausted by the threats. When he had joined this vessel, he had known that it was manned by a crew of cut-throats, but he had been given no say in the matter. Lady Bracknell used the *Albatross* to conduct her opium trade with her contacts in the Orient so was not picky about the men on board. All that she required was that they did the job, no questions asked. 'But I think they're serious about shooting me if you don't do as they ask.'

Dismissing the sailor with a contemptuous toss of her head, Eve sat cross-legged at the bars. 'I don't understand. Why do they do this? I have cleared a passage for your ship. You are pleased, no?'

Mel wondered if she knew much about men and their twisted plans. 'Yes, I'm pleased. I didn't want to die here. Thank you.'

Ewan settled down on a low stool, keeping both Eve and Mel in sight.

'But they say I must come with you or they kill Boy?' Eve was understandably bewildered.

Mel shrugged. 'It looks that way.'

Eve wrinkled her lopsided brow, one side out of line with the other where a seam cut across. 'Why do they do this?'

'Because they can.' Mel spoke from a vast experience of bullying.

'Because ye, my bonnie beastie,' said Ewan, 'will earn us pots of money. The Queen pays well for curiosities and ye are the most curious of all oddities. The Royal Society only exists to feed her appetite for the marvellous.' He made a great show of checking the barrels of his pistol so she was sure he would use them if she made a sudden move.

Not far from where they were sitting, the engines picked up their pace, sending a tremble through the floor. The *Albatross* was losing no time making use of the escape route Eve had forced to open sea.

'Will you stay?' Mel asked, fearing her answer. There was no reason why an all-powerful creature like her should bow to the demands of this cockroach crew. She could simply stamp on those in her path to freedom – they would have no hope of stopping her. And he would get shot.

'I will not let them kill my friend.' She closed her eyes, flexing her fingers in front of her, still reacquainting herself with their movement after so many years of inactivity. *The whole day must have come as a horrid shock to her*, Mel thought.

'Thank you. For agreeing to stay.' He felt a lump in his throat. No one had ever risked themselves for him like she had.

Ewan gave a humph of approval.

Eve sighed. 'You are welcome, Boy.'

'My name is Mel Foster.'

'You are welcome, Mel Foster.'

The two prisoners sat in silence, one in, one outside the bars. Mel dozed and he thought that perhaps Eve did too. Some hours later, Smerdyakov, a Russian crew member, relieved Ewan as guard. He brought food for the pair and sent Ewan up for his rations. The hum of the engines had evened out, indicating that they had indeed made open sea. Rooting through the contents of her plate, Eve rejected the bacon but nibbled on the ship's biscuit.

'This is good.' She crunched the tough mouthful as if it were crumbly butter shortbread rather than hardtack.

Mel offered her his. 'Swap for the meat?'

She pushed her plate under the bars. 'I do not eat flesh.'

So much for the fears that she would dine on the crew.

'How long have you lived in these parts?' Mel asked, deciding now was as good a time as any to find out about his new, and possibly only, friend on board. It was odd how quickly he was getting used to talking to such an extraordinary person: she looked bizarre but had the nicest manners of anyone he could remember meeting.

'All my life.' Eve flicked a weevil out of the biscuit on to the floor.

'Then why do you speak French and not . . . what do they speak round here, Eskimo?'

Swallowing the last piece of biscuit, she brushed the crumbs from her white dress fastidiously. 'For the usual reason. French was my father's language. He was made in Switzerland. He also taught me English and German. I am remembering more and more as I talk. I am good at speaking English, no?'

'Excellent,' Mel agreed.

She smiled at his praise. 'He would be proud to hear that. He said I had many accomplishments. I am the daughter of his heart.'

Mel wondered if he dared ask, but his curiosity was too much for silence. 'How, if I may be so bold, did you come to be . . . um . . . as you are?'

Eve looked down at herself. 'What do you mean? I have always been like this.'

'I mean, where did you come from? How did you grow up? Were you always this strong, even as a baby?'

'I was never a baby. I came like this.'

'I see.' But he didn't see. Not at all.

Eve sighed. 'I explain to my friend, yes?'

Mel nodded cautiously.

'I am made this way, exactly as my father was. His making-father was a clever but also very stupid man called Victor Frankenstein. He did not love his creation as he should. After many bad things happened, Frankenstein died and my father ran away to be alone where no one could hurt him again. He came here where there are no men. This was what my father told me, you understand?'

'Yes. Please go on.' Glancing at their guard, Mel saw that Smerdyakov was picking nits out of his beard and showed no signs that he was eavesdropping. The Russian only understood basic English.

'My father was content to be alone. Fate had decided it would be that way. Then everything changed.' Eve gave one of her terrifyingly gappy smiles. 'A hospital ship fleeing a war hit an iceberg. It was carrying a party of female orphans. My father tried to save them but he was too late: the cold killed them. All he had was a heap of little bodies and the salvaged ruins of the ship. He was sad that these girls would have no life.

He howled at the skies and scolded the sea for doing this to them. That was when he remembered that he had his maker's notebooks, a record of Frankenstein's experiments. Maybe, he thought, if he could repeat the process that brought him to life, he could save one out of the many that had been lost. So he laboured for many days until he created me. The remains he sent out to sea on a lifeboat from the wreck, set alight as they did to warriors of old. It was a fitting funeral for such generous souls.' Eve took a drink of water. 'Then he waited.'

'Waited for what?' asked Mel breathlessly.

'For the right storm. He needed to animate my body with the spark of life – a process that required not only Victor Frankenstein's brilliant scientific work but also the cooperation of the elements. Eventually, the storm came and I awoke. I was received into the loving arms of my father. He never let me feel one moment of the rejection he had endured at his waking.'

No wonder parts of Eve didn't seem to match. He knew it was impolite to ask, but he couldn't help pondering how many different individuals had been sewn into the one body.

She held her hands out side by side. They were surprisingly small and delicate for a creature of her strength. The hand on the left had slim oval nails, the one on the right had blunter fingers. 'My father always said I should be proud because I am unique. He said I was beautiful.' She turned her eyes on Mel. 'Am I beautiful, Mel Foster? These sailors have not been kind to me.'

'They haven't been very nice to me either.' Mel rubbed his chin, wondering how to approach the truth. Very carefully, he decided. 'Your father was correct: you are unique. To . . . um . . . creatures of your kind you would be beautiful, I'm sure. It's just that us humans aren't used to girls of your,' *find a nice word and quick*, 'dimensions.'

'But my father is gone; there is no other creature of my kind.'

Well spotted. Mel really didn't want to offend her. 'Then I say: handsome is as handsome does.'

That appeared to satisfy her. She nodded sagely. 'That means you are handsome, Mel Foster, despite being puny and having a funny nose, for you do handsomely.'

Mel touched his snub nose self-consciously. He thought it a bit rich to be criticized by a girl who had been sewn together from spare parts. 'What's wrong with my nose?'

She put her thumb against her own and bent up the end. 'It looks like you did this. And you have dots across it.'

'They're freckles – not dots!'

'But your eyes are nice. Blue like the sky in summer. Your hair too – black, like mine.' She pressed her palms together. 'I don't like your Captain Mariner; he does not look handsome, and he does not act handsome. He looks like the sea caught him, chewed him up and then threw him back missing a few parts. Not like me. I have all my limbs.' She admired her toes, one foot noticeably larger than the other.

Mel thought it was only fair that she take pride in what she had. If her strength and quick mind were anything to go by, she had been very amply provided for by her father when he made her. 'You're right not to trust the captain.'

She cocked her head and returned his look with a shrewd one of her own. 'Oh, I trust him: I trust him always to act badly.'

The Prince of Wales arrived at Buckingham Palace in a smart coach and four drawn by matching chestnut horses. He was dressed for the Royal Enclosure at Ascot: grey morning coat, spats and a splendid top hat that did a fine job hiding his thinning hair. Assisted by a groom, he manoeuvred his generous frame out of the carriage and climbed the steps, barely registering the bowing of the footmen. Lord Rosebery and Mr Copperfield waited for him on the red carpet under the covered portico.

'Is it really worth disturbing my day at the races for this, Rosebery?' asked the prince, tapping his gold-tipped cane on the ground.

'I fear so, Your Highness.' Lord Rosebery fell into step as they headed for the throne room. 'Her Majesty has not been seen for days.'

'You say this butler personage appears to have a malign influence on her?' The prince passed his cane and hat to a handy flunky.

'Correct, sir. He is the only person she will see and he is doing precious little to encourage her to remember her duties.'

'I'll have it sorted in a trice.' The prince checked his pocket watch. 'I have a filly running in the three o'clock and I intend to be back to see her race.'

Lord Rosebery exchanged a look with Mr Copperfield. Both seriously doubted the prince could solve the crisis so easily. 'Of course, sir.'

The Prince of Wales now took notice of the private secretary. 'Copperfield,' he said with a fond nod. Mr Copperfield had been a favourite of the royal family for many decades, since he showed the Queen's children how to fly kites in the gardens and arranged donkey rides for their amusement. 'No need to announce me. I'll just go straight in. Open the doors.'

Mr Copperfield wrung his hands, looked in horror at what he was doing and clasped them behind him. 'They are locked, sir.'

The prince clicked his fingers at the nearest footman. 'You. Deal with it.'

Nervously, the footman approached the door.

'Hurry up, man, I haven't got all day.'

An angry Prince of Wales was not to be refused. The

footman booted the doors in the middle. They burst apart.

'By Isambard! What is that smell?' Holding his handkerchief over his face, the prince sallied into the room, followed by Mr Copperfield and the prime minister. 'Mummy, Mummy? It's Bertie.' He almost stumbled over the rotting dolphin tail. 'Remove that monstrosity at once!'

Two footmen hurried in to obey.

The prince rounded the huge pool that had been constructed on the marble tiles. It struck him as familiar, though he did not remember the centrepiece being Admiral Nelson, gushing water from the corners of his hat.

'Why have you put a copy of Nelson's statue and the Trafalgar Square fountain in here?' he asked Mr Copperfield. 'This is a throne room, not Kensington Gardens.'

'They are not copies, Your Highness.'

'What!' The prince reeled as he contemplated the destruction done to London's most famous square. 'But I passed it in the coach only a few minutes ago! I swear *someone*'s statue is on top of the column.'

Mr Copperfield coughed. He knew a certain butler's statue now resided on top of the pillar.

'But I did not see the fountain behind all those hoardings advertising Warren's Boot Blacking. Who said you could do this?'

'Mr Burlington's orders, sir.'

'I'll give him orders!' Leaving that distressing detail for later, the prince continued his search. 'Mummy, where are you?'

A door leading to the Queen's private apartments opened and the butler appeared, pushing the sovereign in a bath chair.

'Do not shout, Bertie. We heard you the first time,' the Queen said with no sign her temper had improved. She was an arresting sight: dressed as usual in her widow's crow-black, she had decked herself in what looked like the entire diamond collection of the Crown Jewels. At least six tiaras sat askew on her head, her wrinkled neck was weighed down by necklaces, her arms were hidden by bracelets, and brooches covered her skirts when she had run out of room on her bodice.

'Mummy?' Bertie blinked.

'Of course, it is us. Who else would we be?' She pointed to a spot where she wished to be wheeled so she had a good view of the water-spouting admiral. She didn't seem at all interested in her visitors. 'Why are you here?'

The Prince of Wales now took in the majestic figure of the butler. 'I do not believe we've been introduced,' he said severely.

'I do not believe we have,' agreed Mr Burlington. Today he was inexplicably dressed in an Indian rajah's robes, gold and white with a crimson sash. A jewel-handled dagger curved at his hip. He still had no shirt. The tailors in Savile Row would be weeping, thought Mr Copperfield.

'Bertie, meet Bertie,' the Queen said, introducing the two Alberts to each other with a careless wave.

'You call your butler "Bertie"?' spluttered the prince.

She frowned at him. 'What else would one call him? It is his name.'

On top of the demotion of Nelson from column statue to pool ornament, this was too much for the Prince of Wales. He crumpled. A quick-witted footman managed to catch him in time, sliding a chair under him before he hit the floor.

'Oh dear, Bertie's quite overset. Must be too much sun. He always was a feeble child.' The Queen turned to look up at her butler. 'Are we finished here? One wants to go back to one's pygmy hippo.'

Lord Rosebery hastened forward. 'Your Majesty, please, I beg an audience.'

Queen Victoria settled back in her chair, double chins pillowing her white face. 'Rosebery. Be quick then.'

'I wish to tender my resignation.'

'Accepted. *Now* are we finished?'

'Not quite, ma'am.' Lord Rosebery tugged at his collar. 'Shall I ask Lord Salisbury to wait on you?'

'Whatever for?' The Queen's index finger tapped a restless beat on the arm of her chair.

'Because he is ready to become your prime minister

and form the next government, if Your Majesty so pleases.'

'That will not be necessary.'

'Not necessary!' Lord Rosebery turned an interesting puce colour. 'But, Your Majesty, if you do not ask him to do it, the country will be without a leader.'

'Mummy, please!' groaned Royal Bertie. 'You must act.'

'Oh pish-tush! We do not want another prime minister.' The Queen looked quite disappointed in her menfolk. 'It is all in hand. Bertie, take us back to the hippo.'

Mr Burlington seized the handles and drew the chair in reverse.

'B-but then, whose hands is the country to be in, Mummy?' asked the Prince of Wales plaintively.

'Why, Mr Burlington's, of course. He provided us with a mermaid, so as a reward we have appointed him Chief Butler to the British Empire. Look to him for your orders from now on. Is that quite clear?'

Chapter Five
Monsters for Her Majesty

Three months after escaping the ice, the *Albatross* sailed into Royal Albert Dock, the newest of the shipyards serving London. Pride of the city, it was located several miles downstream from the metropolis, on a big bend in the Thames. The dock boasted the most up-to-date unloading machinery and welcomed steamships: two points in its favour, as the captain had sent word ahead that he had a difficult cargo to handle.

Mel stumbled on deck, eyes dazzled after months of being locked in the brig with a succession of bored guards.

'Easy now, boy.' Ishmael caught him under the elbow before he fell. The crew had manacled Mel's hands behind him so he had no way of catching himself.

As his vision cleared, he saw that the sky was the

usual London autumnal grey. Spits of rain stippled the salt-bleached planks. Ropes strained to the shore, connecting the steamer to its berth. Red-painted cranes surrounded the ship, like huge semaphore flags spelling out the power of the British Empire trade. Dockyard workers waited below, ready to take the ship's cargo in hand once the customs officers were satisfied. The air buzzed with the hum of machinery.

Nearer to Mel, a small group of uniformed officials stood with Mr Wallace, observing Eve like a party of tourists at the Regent's Park Zoo. She sat with her back resting against the smokestack eating an apple, acting as if she had not noticed their excited inspection. Her outstretched legs forced the seamen to make a large detour around her, inconvenient to them and a small rebellion from her that should have alerted them to the fact that she did not intend to go quietly. Denied further visits in the brig, Mel hadn't had a chance to talk freely to her so he had no idea what she was planning. He could not imagine she would agree to what Mr Wallace had in store for her though; the scientist seriously underestimated her intelligence. Mr Wallace, by contrast, continually demonstrated his stupidity. A new proof stood in the centre of the deck: a big metal box, grey, with two large leather straps like a traveller's trunk. Mel could guess it was meant to be a cage. Likelihood of getting Eve inside? Nil.

The captain emerged from his cabin and joined the little party gathered on the deck. 'Gentlemen.' He nodded to the customs agents. 'I see you've met our extraordinary passenger.'

'Indeed, sir!' The senior officer shook hands with Captain Mariner. 'I have sent a telegraph to the Royal Academy. They're sending one of their experts to verify Mr Wallace's discovery but I'm not sure how fast they'll be. They have their hands full of strange creatures at the moment – bit of a backlog.'

'What?' Wallace's proud demeanour wilted. 'You mean she's not the first?'

'Good lord, no. Ever since the Chief Butler took over, monsters have been discovered throughout the Empire, cropping up in the most unlikely places. There were a couple of werewolves teaching at Harrow, would you believe it? But I've not seen a giantess before, so you may still be in for a reward.'

'Wallace!' growled Captain Mariner.

'You can't blame me if science advanced in my absence,' blustered the man.

Mel glanced over at the distant skyline of London. It seemed much had changed since he sailed six months ago. If he'd heard the officer right, the extraordinary had become an everyday discovery.

'Until the expert arrives,' continued the official, 'I suggest you offload your cargo and store it in the customs house.'

'All in good time, sir. First we have to arrange the transfer of the passenger,' said Captain Mariner.

The customs officer smiled as if the captain was cracking a capital joke. 'You mean the monster?'

An apple core rocketed across the deck and knocked the customs officer out cold.

Captain Mariner smiled wryly as the junior customs men knelt to revive their chief. 'Did Mr Wallace not mention it? We've found she reacts badly to that name.'

'No one calls me monster,' said Eve firmly.

The captain turned to address her. 'Now, creature, it is time for you to leave this vessel. Mr Wallace has constructed you a comfortable box in which you may lie undisturbed as you are moved.' He levered up the lid of the metal trunk. Inside it was padded with straw-filled sacking but it had leather straps fixed at neck, wrist, waist and ankle heights. To Mel's eyes, it was an instrument of torture.

He was not alone in that opinion. Eve took one look at the interior and folded her arms. '*Non*.'

The captain mirrored her gesture. 'Then we shoot the boy.'

'Oh, I say!' exclaimed the recovering customs officer. He had a bump the size of a hen's egg on his forehead. 'Shooting the cabin boy: now that's just not cricket!'

'This is a working steamship, sir, not the playing

fields of Eton,' snapped the captain. 'The boy is the only way we have of controlling the m– mademoiselle.' He stumped over to Mel and hooked him by the shirt front, lifting him off his feet. Eve stood up, fists clenched. 'See: she watches over him like a mother does a baby.'

'Leave Mel Foster alone,' hissed Eve.

Mel turned his face from Captain Mariner's foul breath. Pickled herrings were the least of the odours. He was fed up of being used against Eve but couldn't think of how he could escape.

The captain shook Mel, snapping his head to and fro on his neck. 'Only if you get in there, creature.'

Eve bit her lip, white teeth on grey. Mel had never seen that expression on her face: she was attempting to look timid. 'I cannot. I'm scared of small places.'

'Then I put a bullet in the boy,' said the captain, cocking his pistol and holding it at point-blank range against Mel's left knee.

Eve held up her hands. 'Please, captain. Show me it is safe.'

Mr Wallace edged closer to the captain. 'What harm would it do, sir? She sounds as though she is willing to get in if we prove it to her.'

'That's what I'm worried about.' The captain held Eve's gaze, trying to fathom her motives but his sounding came up without plumbing the depth of her cunning. 'Put the boy in the box.'

Ewan and Ishmael lifted Mel off the captain's hook and carried him over to the trunk.

'See, beastie, he goes in here nice and snug.' Ewan undid one side of Mel's manacles. 'Ye strap the wrists here and here so he doesna get rattled aboot. Nice tight band round the waist and, hey presto, the laddie is ready for transport.'

'And the trunk is thick?' asked Eve, moving closer. She tapped the side with her knuckles. 'Bulletproof?'

'Aye.'

'Shut the lid and show me that he can still breathe.'

As Ewan and Ishmael closed the top, Eve caught Mel's eye and winked. Puzzled, he smiled back to reassure her. Mel had plenty of room – it had been built for Eve's much larger frame, so he didn't feel claustrophobic. The voices outside could still be heard through the air holes drilled in the lid near his head. They also let in a faint light.

'Thank you. I agree, it is safe,' said Eve pleasantly. 'I will be leaving now.'

Mel felt the trunk swing up from the deck and come to rest on the back of the giantess. He sank down a little but the bindings held him upright. He realized that Eve had gripped the box by the straps. With three bounds, she now ran for the side.

'Quick, lads, she's escaping!' roared the captain.

Guns went off, bullets ricocheting from the metal trunk. Clever, clever Eve! Knowing she couldn't do anything while Mel was still vulnerable, she had wrapped him in the armoured box meant to contain her.

Then they went airborne. Mel's heart was in his mouth. The box jolted when it landed in the water, making Mel glad for the padding. But the air holes that had provided him with light and air now threatened to be the death of him. Water sprayed in, hitting his face then trickling down to rest at the bottom by his feet. Mel could do nothing to warn Eve that her escape plan had a serious flaw. Perhaps she didn't know that ordinary humans needed to breathe?

This is it: my new bad end. He couldn't even scream without taking a mouthful of filthy Thames. He turned his face to one side so that he now had to endure the lesser torture of the water pouring in his ear.

Then the box heaved upwards and light replaced the water. With a *thunk*, the box landed on the ground and Mel was lying on his back. Water sloshed around him, reaching halfway up his body. The lid was thrown back and Eve grinned down at him. She was soaking wet and streaked with mud, sleek like a huge otter.

'Are you unhurt, Mel Foster?'

'Get me out!' he pleaded. He couldn't bear the idea of remaining there a moment longer.

Gunshots pinged off the lid. Mel now noticed that

Eve had been hit in the upper arm, but blood was only flowing sluggishly from the wound.

'First I get us out of range.'

The next thing Mel heard were male screams and pleading. Then a nearby engine started and the box juddered. Mel realized that they were on another boat, possibly a tug from the powerful growl of the engines. He heard a splash and felt the surging sensation of moving at full speed ahead. Eve opened the box again and reached in. She snapped the straps, not bothering with the buckles, then lifted Mel out, standing him upright. She crumbled the manacle off his wrist and threw it over the side.

'There. We escaped.' She gave him a grin which he could not help but return. Flinching a little, she squeezed her arm and a flattened bullet popped out. The bleeding had already stopped.

Mel was overcome with gratitude. 'Eve, you were brilliant.'

She blew on her nails and polished them on her filthy dress. 'I know. It helped that they were stupid.'

He laughed, drunk with happiness at their escape. 'So, what next?'

'I do not know.' Eve took the wheel. 'Which way?'

Mel now had a chance to look about him. The tugboat was beetling up the river. In its wake was the bobbing shape of the tugboat pilot, appealing for someone to come and save him. That explained the splash.

Eve shrugged. 'I said he could jump after he started her running. Now you tell me where we go.'

Mel scratched his head. Where could they flee and not be noticed? Downstream were the marshes, but they offered little in the way of food and shelter. Upstream was a city of a million souls, a place he knew well. 'I think we stand the best chance if we disappear into the streets of London. We're heading that way already.' To port was the green hill of Greenwich Park and the Royal Observatory. In a little while, they would come to Tower Bridge. There were plenty of places to disembark on the northern and southern banks. 'But first we need to disguise you.' Even if extraordinary creatures really had become an everyday occurrence, he still thought Eve was likely to turn heads.

Eve held up a man's raincoat and floppy hat that had been dropped on the deck. 'The pilot took these off before he jumped. Will these do?'

'They'll do nicely.' Mel took over the wheel while Eve tried on her new wardrobe. She pulled the hat's brim low; covered by the coat she looked almost normal, if you ignored her bare feet and hands.

The tug rounded a bend in the river, revealing the majestic towers of the new bridge.

Eve's mouth dropped open. '*Sacré bleu, c'est magnifique!*'

Of course: Eve had never seen a building bigger than an igloo. 'It's Tower Bridge – only just finished. The bit in the middle lifts to let tall ships pass through.'

'It is wonderful. I like. I like very much.'

They passed under the central span as omnibuses and carriages clattered overhead. Practiced in river navigation thanks to Ishmael's tutoring on the *Albatross*, Mel guided the tug between other vessels, trying to hide among the hundreds of boats out on the Thames. Not for a second did he think they were completely free of pursuit, though Eve had chosen well when she had pirated this vessel: its top speed matched the fastest boats on the river. It would take the crew a while to catch up.

Unlike Mel, Eve was less concerned about those who would be chasing them. Her attention was now struck by the Tower of London with its ancient pale stone walls, then the wharves and storehouses of the south bank. She rushed from port to starboard taking in her first impressions of the city. The North Pole may have been a safe retreat for her and her father, but clearly it had also lacked the variety to satisfy Eve's curiosity.

Mel had long since lost his wonder at the buildings of London and tea-coloured Thames. Squeers's Orphanage had been little more than a money-making venture for its owner, though he hid the fact from his board of governors. He regarded the boys as a flock to be farmed and then sold on to new owners. As soon as Mel could walk, he had been sent out to earn his bed and board as a crossing sweeper, a label paster in a blacking factory and later as an undertaker's boy until Lady Bracknell had intervened. But that early training had an unexpected benefit: he knew the warren of city streets and he had some hope that he could hide Eve for a time until they came up with a better plan for their survival. His old life as cabin boy was over. From the moment he had woken Eve, there had been no going back.

'Mel Foster, are there always so many people in London?' asked Eve.

Mel glanced up at the fancy ironwork of Southwark Bridge. A row of faces lined the rail; in places onlookers were standing three deep. 'Yes, but they don't usually stand there.' He could hear shrill police whistles and shouts. 'I think they're expecting us.'

Eve pulled her hat lower over her face. 'How can that be? We have left the sailors behind. How can those that hunt us now be ahead?'

Mel realized that there was a big gap in her education. She knew the world as her father had left it at the beginning of the century. Much had changed since then. 'There's this invention called the telegraph, Eve. Messages are sent by wire. That allows word to fly ahead of even the fastest boat.'

She looked sceptical.

'You don't need to understand how it works, just that I think we'd better get off the river. Even with the other boats, a stolen tug is too easy to spot.' He directed the prow towards the dome of St Paul's, intending to disembark in one of the narrow alleys between the warehouses on the waterfront. Mel nudged the tug between two coal barges and gestured to Eve to head for the shore, pulling her brim low to hide her features.

A coal heaver in his blackened clothes and battered hat stood on the quay, smoking a pipe. He watched them with interest but no alarm as they clambered over the coal he had come to fetch. Police whistles could still be heard in the distance.

'What's all that about, sir?' asked Mel, wondering how far news of their escape had travelled.

'Ach, some bother with the MPs.' The coal heaver spat into the water.

That wasn't the answer Mel had been expecting. 'Members of Parliament?'

The man laughed, his mouth very pink against his coal-stained skin. 'Nay, lad, where you been these last few months? There ain't no parliament no longer. The new MPs are the Monster Patrolmen. They've done away with the coppers too. Queen's orders, they say.'

'Oh yes. Yes, of course.' Mel pushed Eve gently in the back to steer her up the alleyway. He noticed that the old bills on the grimy brick walls had been covered with new posters:

WANTED
DEAD OR ALIVE

MONSTERS
FOR HER MAJESTY

GOOD PRICES GIVEN
FOR THE BEST SPECIMENS

SIGNED *Albert Burlington,*
CHIEF BUTLER

So the customs officer was right: there must be more extraordinary creatures like Eve coming to light and there was even a new police force to round them up. But what did this cove Burlington want with so many specimens? Nothing good, Mel feared.

'We must get off the streets. This way, before anyone gets a close look at you.' He beckoned Eve to follow him between two warehouses. Rain was falling more heavily now, driving most people off the streets. Eve enjoyed the puddles forming in the potholed roadway and splashed in as many as she could. Mel supposed that, coming from the frozen north, rain was a novelty. It wouldn't take long in London to cure her of that.

They had reached Distaff Lane when the whistles caught up with them.

'There they are!' someone shouted.

Mel glanced behind and saw three men in uniform running up the road towards them, blowing police whistles. They wore bright red tunics with red trousers, gun holsters, and leather sashes across their chests with the words 'Monster Patrol' stamped on them. Their scarlet helmets had a badge with a pitchfork in the centre.

'Quick!' Mel took Eve's hand and dashed between the carriages rattling along St Paul's Churchyard. Their speed caused Eve's hat to flap back, giving a shocked cabbie a glimpse of her face. He drove his hansom cab right into a milk cart, causing a collision of multiple vehicles.

'Where are we going, Mel Foster?' asked Eve. She did not sound the least winded, whereas Mel's breaths were puffing like bellows.

'We're taking sanctuary . . . in there.' He pointed to the cathedral. The once-white stone of the huge building was now a sooty black, but the grey dome still rose above all the other buildings, fighting for dominance of the upper airs only with the murk that was settled permanently over the city.

'I carry you.' Eve grabbed Mel around the waist and threw him over her shoulder. Bouncing along in a fireman's lift, Mel could see that they had not shaken their pursuers. Eve leapt lightly up the steps leading to the main doors. Her hat fell off, held on round her neck only by its strings. Screams and shouts added to the whistles behind them, and the terrified cathedral vergers hurried to close the entrance. The huge doors shut with a boom a second before she could go through.

'Mel Foster, they do not want us.' Eve now craned her head, looking upward. 'We go in by the first floor. Hold on tight!'

Before he could protest, she jumped, just managing to grab on to the ledge over the first row of columns. Mel closed his eyes: looking down gave him a vertiginous glimpse of the steps below. Eve swung for a moment one-armed, checking that Mel was still balanced on her shoulder, then heaved them on to the balcony under the ornate portico.

The doors up here were also closed.

'I can break them open,' offered Eve, putting Mel down on his feet. He rubbed his aching stomach.

He had revised his opinion about the likelihood of being offered sanctuary. Desperate but still determined to save his friend, he searched his memory for another hiding place. 'I don't think we're welcome inside, Eve. We need to get away from the patrol and think where to go next.'

A bullet chipped the column next to Eve's head. The Monster Patrol had caught up with them.

'We can't stay here.' Eve looked over the edge, unperturbed by the shots.

'Can bullets kill you?' Mel asked, concerned she didn't know the danger.

Eve plucked another missile out of her hair. This one had barely broken her skin. 'I do not think so. But they can kill you. We must go higher. Climb on my back.'

Relieved to be upright, Mel clung to her, piggyback style.

'I will climb a column on this side. I only have to leave cover for a second as I swing on to the roof.' Eve had already started her ascent as she explained her plan. 'Hold very tightly!' she warned as she stretched out to grip the roof edge. The architect had thoughtfully provided a broad ledge at this point on the facade so she was able to climb across with no slips. They were now on the roof. The cathedral was built in the shape of a cross. The broad slopes of the tiles over the nave, the long part of the cross, stretched before them, as big as a football pitch. The gallery and dome appeared even bigger from here, like a round church cadging a ride on its bigger brother below.

'If we get to the other end,' suggested Mel, wiping the rain from his eyes, 'we might be able to climb down into the churchyard and make our escape that way.'

The roof of the nave was simple to navigate; getting past the dome was another challenge. As they neared it, Mel saw that their hunters had climbed to the Whispering Gallery, the lower section under the dome, and were waiting for them behind the stone columns.

He tugged the back of her coat. 'Eve, we've got company.' He risked a glance over the side of the parapet. The road around the cathedral had been closed and cleared. Military and Monster Patrolmen were gathering, swarming like red ants.

Eve did not seem worried. 'Then we go higher.' She squinted at the Stone Gallery that ran over the top of the Whispering one and was just under the dome. No men had reached that yet. 'I can jump from there to the other side where there is more roof like this, yes?'

Mel nodded. There was a similar roof over the shorter quire of the cathedral, the top of the cross. 'You can, but they're going to shoot at us.'

'I know, Mel Foster. Put your arms around my neck and hold on like monkey. My body will shelter yours.'

Mel climbed aboard, winding his legs around her waist.

She looked down at him and smiled. 'You are very good friend, Mel Foster.'

He smiled but there was a lump in his throat. Even though she would have a better chance of escape without him, she gave no hint she considered abandoning him. She was a top-class giantess.

'Ready?' she asked.

'Yes.'

With a run, she broke cover and dashed for the columns. Guns fired. Whistles screeched. She heaved herself up the first pillar through the sheer strength of her bare hands and feet, like the South Sea Islanders shinning up coconut trees. Eve reached the Stone Gallery and dived over the rail. She lay there for a moment, rain dripping on her face, chest heaving. Mel felt her shaking under him. He rolled off, worried for her, but then he saw that she was laughing.

'That was fun, no?' Eve sat up and pushed her hair off her brow.

'That wasn't the word I was thinking of.'

'Let's go.' She pulled Mel along with her to the far side of the gallery. They were now on the east side of St Paul's. Eve was exhilarated at outwitting her pursuers and eager to continue. 'There is the other roof just as you said. I jump.' She scooped Mel up again.

'But . . .' He did not have time to get his words out.

He had seen movement down among the tombstones but Eve was already on the parapet.

'Hold tight!' she said.

She leapt.

Boom! Hidden behind a lavish monument, a field gun fired. The shell collided with Eve and Mel, Eve taking the brunt of the impact. In her shock she dropped Mel and cartwheeled in the air, carried off on the same trajectory as the missile. That was the last Mel saw of her before he hit the roof.

Chapter Six
Blood Donor

It was the bed that first came to his attention. Mel was cushioned on a mattress, head on a pillow. He had not slept with a pillow in either the orphanage or at sea, so he couldn't work out where he was. Then, as more senses returned, he discovered that he hurt. Everywhere. There was a heavy sensation across his chest. By wiggling his fingers, he realized it had to be his left arm, strapped to a splint. His left leg felt exceedingly heavy so that was probably also broken. Woozily, he turned his head slightly to the side and opened his eyes. On the bedside table stood a white enamel basin and jug with *St Bartholomew's* stamped in blue ink across them. That answered one question: somehow he had gone from cathedral roof to hospital. But where was Eve?

Just as he was about to panic, there was a flutter

at the window and a girl appeared at his bedside. Mel guessed he had to be dazed because he hadn't seen her walk in; it seemed as though the air had just thickened and there she was. Strange. His bed was in a room on its own and he had not noticed the door open since he woke up. Still, it was getting dark. Perhaps she was on night duty and had been waiting in the shadows for him to return to consciousness?

'Hello. Are you a nurse?' His voice sounded very rough.

She slipped a cool hand under his head and held a glass to his lips. 'Here: drink.'

He took a few gulps, trying to make sense of what had happened to him. The nurse was watching him with quiet interest. Even in the twilight, he could see that she was very pretty: face delicate like a daisy petal, long wavy golden hair, sapphire-blue eyes, red lips. Now he came to think about it, she didn't look very much like a nurse. Not only was she far too young – about his age, he would guess – but she wasn't in uniform. He was sure she wouldn't be allowed to go about her duties with her hair unbound like that.

'I'm sorry, miss, but who are you?'

She put the glass on the bedside table. Every movement she made was like ballet, carefully choreographed and elegantly executed. 'I am called Viorica.' Her voice was soothing, lightly accented like the eastern European sailors he knew.

He was beginning to feel sleepy again but he couldn't pass out, not until he understood what was happening. 'That's a nice name, miss. Where's it from?'

She smoothed the hair off his face, her fingers running down the side of his neck, checking his pulse. 'From Transylvania.'

Mel felt his lids grow heavy. 'What are you doing here, Miss Viorica?'

'Don't worry, English boy. I am merely here to do a blood transfusion.'

Mel tried to rouse himself. Something wasn't right. This was a risky new procedure, only done in emergencies. 'But I didn't lose any blood, did I?'

'This transfusion is from you to me.' She opened her mouth to reveal two sharp white fangs.

'No!' Mel thrust her away but moving had turned treacly. He could feel her eager fingers gripping his shoulders, her hot breath on his neck. 'Don't bite me! Help!'

Just as the tips of her fangs broke skin, the window smashed inwards. Eve swung into the room, letting go of a rope of knotted bedsheets to land with a thump.

'Move away from the boy!' She was furious, black hair whipping about her like snakes.

Viorica was too caught up in the scent of blood to pull back, her eyes glowing like hot coals. She took one gulp. Pain streaked through Mel's throat.

'*Arrête*!' Eve lifted Viorica bodily away and threw

her across the room, but instead of smashing into the brickwork, the girl used it as a springboard to catapult herself at the giantess. The two crashed into the wall, sending the basin and jug flying. Eve shoved the girl in the chest, aiming for the window. Viorica spun in mid-air, gripped the window frame and swung back, pointed feet targeting Eve's face. Eve ducked and grabbed a handful of her hair. She whirled Viorica into the door with a crunch that left a dent in the wood. Mel was amazed that the little blonde girl hadn't been crushed, but Viorica was snarling, spitting like a cat, still very much in fighting form. Pouncing on Eve, she opened her mouth wide and tried to sink her teeth in Eve's throat.

'Ow!' Viorica leapt away from Eve, hopping in agony, checking her fangs were still in place. 'What are you?' She delicately pressed the tip of one tooth. 'You are like marble!'

Eve stood between the bed and Viorica, quivering with anger. 'I am Mel Foster's friend. You will not hurt him.'

Viorica seemed to shrink back to the elegant little girl she had first appeared to be, but Mel was no longer fooled. She shrugged. 'But I was not going to hurt him.' Mel dabbed at the trickle of blood running down his chest, the movement catching Viorica's attention. 'Well, not so much. Not to kill him.'

Eve stabbed a blunt finger at her. 'You eat his neck!'

'Ugh!' Viorica looked genuinely disgusted at the accusation. 'I do not eat flesh; I just suck his blood, a little sip to quench me.' She brushed her mouth, lips cherry-stained. 'I'm still thirsty.' Her blue eyes glittered with their fiery gleam again.

'You will not drink from Mel Foster.' Eve folded her arms. 'Understood?'

Reluctantly, Viorica nodded. 'I will not feed from him while you are here.'

They all heard the threat: she would return to his neck the moment Eve left.

'What are you?' whispered Mel. He thought he could guess. He had read about creatures like her, and if monsters were abroad then . . . 'Why do you want to hurt me?'

Viorica slid further into the shadows. Eve strode after her and grabbed her wrist, dragging her back into the moonlight.

'*Non*, you will not leave until you explain. Tell the boy what you are.'

'It is nothing personal,' said Viorica without a hint of apology. 'I'm a vampire, Mel Foster. You eat meat; I drink blood. I do not understand why people find that so shocking.'

'But my father told me you exist forever and can transform into many creatures – explain that to the boy.' Eve turned to look at Mel. 'Do not trust her, Mel Foster; vampires are the undead. They hate the living.'

Viorica snapped her long fingers. 'Absurd. I do not hatc the living; I love the way they taste.' She tried to free her wrist. 'But what are *you*? I've not met one of you before.' She sniffed. 'You do not smell human but yet you seem rather like a very large one. I do not understand you.'

Mel decided it was high time for him to escape the hospital before Eve had to leave and Viorica returned to thoughts of dinner. His arm was in a sling and his leg was splinted but he thought he could probably walk with Eve's help. He slid out of bed on the far side, noticing that he had been put in a baggy grey striped nightshirt and had no shoes.

Eve moved to shield his movements from Viorica's hungry gaze. 'I am Eve Frankenstein. I am unique.'

Viorica's eyes went back to her. 'Yes, I see that. You must tell me about yourself. I enjoy stories about monsters.'

'I am not a monster!'

'No?' Viorica smiled. 'Well, I am – and proud of it.' She curtsied. 'Lady Viorica Dracula, delighted to meet you.'

'Dracula?' Even Mel had heard that name. Count Dracula had run amok in Whitby and London just a couple of years ago. The papers had been full of the horrors he had committed: killing an entire ship's crew, turning innocent maidens into deranged blood-drinking brides, murdering many until some brave people defeated him. The newspapers had claimed he was just a madman, unwilling to confirm what others were whispering: that he was really a vampire.

'Yes. My brother was the famous Count, but I've always believed it prudent to keep in the shadows.' She gave a little philosophical shake of the head. 'Look at him: he courted public attention and got staked for his trouble.'

'So now you haunt the hospital, taking blood from those too weak to resist you?' asked Mel, despising her.

'Only the most hopeless cases who won't notice it.' Viorica's eyes drifted to the trail of blood running down his nightshirt.

Mel clapped his right hand over the stain. 'I'm not hopeless! There's not much wrong with me!'

'Physically, no, you will mend if you are given the chance. But you are wanted by the Monster Patrol and people who fall into their hands do not come back. I thought I'd take advantage before they got to you. They will be here in the morning to take you to the Chief Butler.' She shuddered. 'Now, there is one whom I really would not like to bite.'

Mel located his boots under the bed. He hooked them out with the toes of his good foot. All the more reason to run for it.

'I don't understand. What is a Chief Butler?' asked Eve.

Viorica smoothed her hair behind her perfect little

ear; in the lobe a ruby stud glinted like a drop of blood. 'He is in charge now. He has taken over the British Empire.'

'But what about the government – the Queen?' asked Mel.

'The government has gone; the Queen is under his spell.' Viorica tried to ease her wrist from Eve's grip. 'He is gathering all of us at the Palace. None of us know what happens once we go inside, except that, if any of us resist, we don't come out.'

Eve frowned. 'Who are "us"?'

Viorica gave another of her shrugs. 'I mean us monsters who are free. Before the Chief Butler came to power, we only had to hide from the few humans who believed in our existence. If we kept quiet, we were safe. Now our presence is known, all are on the lookout and we have to shelter in secret places from everyone, especially the Monster Patrol. They are very good at finding those he has put on his list.' She turned to Mel, a sad little smile of commiseration on her lips. 'I am sorry, Mel Foster, but I heard the nurses say that you are on that list, which means you are doomed. Are you sure you don't want to give me a little of your blood, as you won't be needing it?' She edged closer.

'Really sure, thanks,' said Mel. 'Eve, we've got to run.' He stood up, using the bed for support. He wished he was facing this dressed in more than a nightshirt.

Eve wrinkled her brow. 'You have a plan?'

'No. But I'll think of one.'

'Your best chance is to leave him, Mademoiselle Frankenstein. He will slow you down.' Viorica licked her lips. 'I could promise to look after him for you.'

'I would prefer to leave him with this Chief Butler,' said Eve stoutly.

'No, you really would not,' replied Viorica, deadly serious.

Mel heard voices in the courtyard below the window. Eve's noisy entrance had not gone unnoticed. Terror rattled about inside him like bone dice in a gambler's cup. None of the throws looked promising. Running was best.

'Please, Eve, let's go.'

'*Oui*, we go.' She picked up Mel, taking care not to jolt his broken limbs. 'And you too, Lady Dracula.' With less care, she bundled Viorica under the other arm.

'Put me down, imbecile!' snarled Viorica, leaving niceness behind now she sensed Eve's intention to keep her captive. 'I can fly out of here.'

The sounds had reached the corridor outside Mel's room.

'Maybe you can, but you save us first.' Eve went to the window and stepped on to the sill.

'Eve, remember what happened last time!' warned Mel. He didn't have many more limbs to break.

Something odd was happening to Viorica. Her shape was turning vague and sparkly. Her eyes were darkening, ears growing, arms twig-like, brown hair covering her skin.

'*Non*, vampire. If you transform, I bruise your batwings so you no more fly for a week!' growled Eve.

Viorica's transformation stopped. Bitter blue eyes once more glared at Eve from under her arm.

'No one should be as strong as you!' Viorica snapped.

'And no one should be as bloodthirsty as you. Hold tight.' As the door to the room opened, Eve launched herself from the window.

And landed lightly in the courtyard. Whistles and rattles sounded overhead. Mel got a brief glimpse of faces crowded at the window before Eve loped into the darkness of the street beyond the hospital. Pistols exploded but the only damage was taken by the stone arch they passed through. Eve ran on, not pausing for breath even though she was carrying two passengers, and one of them very unwilling.

'So, what is it to be, Lady Dracula? I can continue running until the Patrolmen catch us all, or you can direct me to your secret place.'

'Never!' spat Viorica.

Eve smiled grimly. 'I could hide Mel Foster inside this church and turn us both in. I don't think the Patrolmen would be so interested in him if they had us, do you?' It started to rain heavily, helping disguise their escape. Eve leapt the iron fence around a little city chapel, dodging among the glistening tombs. Angels wept. Crosses lurched sideways. Ivy covered the names of the dead. Taking cover from the deluge, she stopped in the porch and lowered Mel to the damp stone floor. She patted him on the head. 'You seek sanctuary here, Mel Foster, when the priest comes in the morning.'

Mel opened his mouth to protest but the barest wink from Eve shut off his words.

Viorica hit Eve's arm to gain her attention. The vampire was shivering like someone struck down with a sudden fever. Her already pale skin had gone the shade of skimmed milk, white touched with blue, ghastly under the faint moonlight. 'Take me away. I cannot enter a church.'

'Why? What happens if you do?' Despite her attack on him, Mel felt a little sorry for her: she looked so stricken. It was hard not to believe her sweet innocent appearance.

'Please!'

Eve took a step away from the porch but did not let go of her captive. 'Better?'

Viorica nodded, pearly teeth sinking into her lip. They had reached a stalemate.

'Why will you not help us?' Mel asked. 'Eve and I mean you no harm. We just want to seek refuge in your hideout.'

Viorica shut her eyes. 'I have only just found safety and I promised the others. There are rules.'

'But that is no problem,' said Eve. 'We won't betray

your secret. We can promise too. I have found Mel Foster to be a very honourable boy, and a Frankenstein never goes back on a vow.'

Behind her, Mel glimpsed a light beyond the iron palings – a lantern swinging to and fro, hard to see in the downpour. He tugged Eve's coat.

She waved him away. 'Moment, Mel Foster, I am speaking with the vampire.'

Mel scowled, annoyed that Eve was ignoring him at this crucial moment.

'But no ordinary human is allowed where I live. They will kill him,' whispered Viorica.

'Then I stop them.'

'Eve! Look!' insisted Mel.

Above the patter of rain, a whistle pierced the night: they had been spotted.

Eve picked up Mel. 'Choose now, Lady Dracula: deal with your friends' anger or deal with mine.'

With a hiss of a breath, Viorica blurted out an address in a fashionable part of London. 'I will not be responsible for what happens, understood?'

'*Bien sûr*. Mel Foster, can you direct?' Eve was not yet ready to trust the vampire to lead her without trying a trick or two.

Well versed in London streets from his days as a crossing sweeper, Mel reeled off the directions. Eve broke into a run, splashing through puddles, striding over the gravestones like a hurdler. Shouts came from the far side of the churchyard: their pursuers had not yet given up. They had to get off the gaslit streets so they could lose their hunters in the dark.

'Down there!' Mel pointed to a dank back alley that would lead them to Bloomsbury off the main routes.

Eve plunged into the darkness. A cat's eyes flared briefly in the shadows before it disappeared over a wall. The sounds of pursuit were more distant now. Eve's breath came strong and steady. Mel took comfort from that, trying not to get too anxious about their destination. It was no good: if Viorica was afraid of the others who lived in her house, then he knew he should be very worried. With a sinking sense of dread, Mel directed Eve right to the door of the house Viorica had named. The rain eased off briefly, leaving them shivering on the step.

'This is your hideout?' asked Mel dubiously. Was it a trap? It looked more like the home of a gentleman of means: freshly painted black front door, scrubbed white step, rich red-brocade curtains at the wide windows, spiked iron railings setting it apart from the street. Nice digs for a nest of vampires.

Viorica did not answer. She appeared to be dealing with him by ignoring his presence.

'Go on: knock,' urged Eve.

Still in her undignified position under one arm, Viorica found herself lifted up by Eve and nudged towards the door, much like a brass-topped walking stick in a gentleman's hand. Muttering darkly, Viorica reached out and rapped the knocker. Only then did Mel notice that it was shaped like a human skull.

With no signs of anyone having answered it, the door swung open. Eve didn't hesitate: she entered and kicked it closed with her heel. The boom echoed throughout the house. Her muddy bare feet looked barbaric on the chequered floor tiles of the entrance hall, toenails yellow against the cool white.

'Now will you put me down?' snapped Viorica.

Gently, Eve lowered Mel to sit on a wooden chest against one wall. She then tossed Viorica free, like a bowler releasing a cricket ball. Placing herself in front of Mel, Eve stood ready to repel the next attack. There was no need: Viorica was too bruised by her inelegant passage across town to risk coming near Eve again. She somersaulted, transforming into a bat mid-spin, her empty dress flopping to the ground in a soggy heap. With a high-pitched screech of fury, she fluttered once around Eve's head, then spiralled up into the darkness of the stairwell.

Mel blinked. He'd just watched a girl turn into a bat. Never in a million years had he anticipated seeing such a sight.

'Did she . . .?'

'*Oui*.' Eve sighed and put her hands on her hips, trying to spot Viorica above them.

'I don't think she likes us.' Mel rubbed his broken

arm with his right hand, checking it had taken no more damage. He did not really feel safe even though the door was closed on the Patrolmen. 'Are you sure this is the hideout? She might have tricked us.'

'Yes, she might.' Eve turned to smile at him in reassurance. 'But we are safe for now, no?'

'I wouldn't be certain of that, if I were you.' A new voice spoke from the landing overhead. The person's tone was boyish, refined: the kind of speech Mel only heard from the young, rich visitors to the orphanage, the ones that came to gloat at the poor unfortunates. 'I suggest you leave now, before you have to deal with us.'

Eve searched the shadows, bristling at the challenge. '*Non*, we will not.'

'Ah me, such a pity. Then I had better come down and sort out the mess Lady Dracula has dragged in. This won't end well – for either of you.'

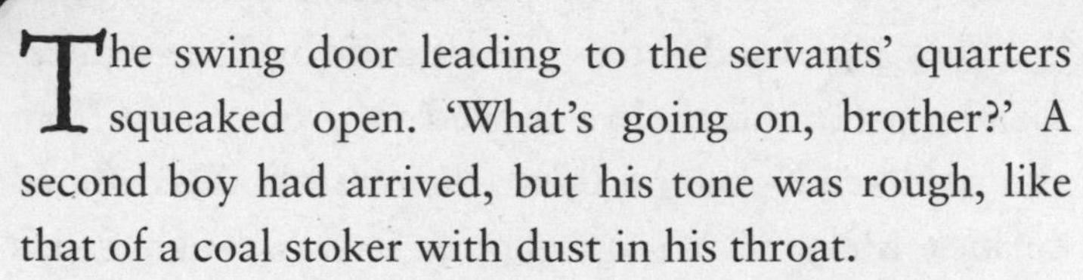

Chapter Seven
Cain and Abel

The swing door leading to the servants' quarters squeaked open. 'What's going on, brother?' A second boy had arrived, but his tone was rough, like that of a coal stoker with dust in his throat.

A slim young gentleman of about fifteen appeared on the stairs carrying a candle. He was dressed for bed in green silk pyjamas and had thrown a paisley satin robe over his clothes. His thick chestnut hair looked ruffled, flattened slightly on one side where he had been lying. His shrewd green eyes inspected the visitors.

'Unfortunately, Cain, our newest recruit, Lady Dracula, has broken the rules of our haven. She has delivered one damp monster – you are very welcome, miss – but also one filthy street urchin – you, boy, are not.'

'Hah! Shall I kick him out?' The gruff speaker shuffled into view. His arms were long for his body and his back bent, giving him an ape-like stance. His brown hair sprouted in wild tufts. He looked the same age as his brother but his movements were much clumsier, like boys in the orphanage who had hit a growth spurt and hadn't had time to get used to their new strength.

'I fear this large young lady might object if we do that.' The young gentleman with the candle had reached the ground floor. His gaze met his brother's. Unexpectedly, he puffed out the flame, leaving them in shadows. Grunts and groans came from the foot of the stairs.

'Eve, what's happening?' whispered Mel.

'They plan something – something bad,' she replied. Sizing up the threat, Eve moved to protect him from the ape-like boy behind them, the one who had offered to kick Mel out. Wrong choice. It was rough hands from the *front* that seized Mel, coming from where the elegant boy had been standing. Had the ape-like brother jumped right over them in the darkness and evaded Eve that way? No matter how it had been done, Mel found himself dragged across the floor. He cried out as his broken leg jolted.

'Mel Foster!' yelled Eve. 'Give him back!'

But too late: Mel was pulled swiftly backwards out of the foyer like a partridge carried to the hunters by the gun dog. A door slammed somewhere behind him.

'Please! My leg: it's broken!'

'Stop squealing!' grunted his abductor, breathing

heavily as he hauled Mel away. Mel could feel calloused knuckles gripping his collar, digging into the back of his neck. He was taken outside across a small courtyard, bumped past herbs in pots and a fountain tinkling into a shell basin, then inside another building, an annex to the main house. The outer door swung closed, leaving Mel alone with his captor.

'Not another bad end,' whispered Mel, groping around for a weapon to defend himself.

A curse came from his abductor, a cry of pain, then silence. Mel counted out his remaining seconds.

'What did you say?' It was the softly spoken tenor again, the young man who had drifted down the staircase like a king in his court, not the gruff one. But how had they changed places so quickly? Mel decided he must have missed something – blacked out for a second. He hoped, however, that the civilised young man would be more reasonable than his terrifying brother.

'Please, sir, I've done nothing to you.'

'Answer me! What did you say?'

Mel gulped. 'I said that this looked like another bad end. Mr Squeers told me I'd meet one.'

The young gentleman laughed, not a reassuring sound.

'I thought it had come when we got stuck in the ice.' The words tumbled from Mel; he had to find the key that would unlock this boy's sympathy. Amusing him was better than nothing. 'And again when I woke up

Eve by mistake, and I really thought it had come today when I fell off St Paul's Cathedral, but now I'm thinking *this* is it.'

The lights went on with a suddenness that took Mel by surprise. Overhead a three-pronged light hung from the ceiling, glass bulbs blazing. Its globe shades were etched with the countries of the world.

'Is that magic?' he asked hoarsely. Nothing would be unthinkable tonight.

'No. Electricity.' The elegant boy leaned back against a desk. There was no sign of his brother. Quickly looking around him for other threats, Mel saw that they were in a workroom, books and equipment piled on all surfaces and shelves. An articulated human skeleton hung from a hook in the far corner, vacant sockets and slack-jawed mouth gaping at the room, but even more frightening was the steel-topped table with channels running down the side leading to a drain in the floor. Mel was sure that very bad things happened on that table. The boy tapped his fingers on the desk edge. 'What are we going to do with you?'

Mel was not so stupid as to think his opinion was being sought.

'I'm Mel Foster,' he said instead. 'Just an orphan. No one who can be a threat to a swell like yourself.'

'You misunderstand, Master Foster. It is enough that you know where we live.' The young gentleman got up and belted his robe around his waist, clearly making a decision. He gave Mel a negligent nod of introduction. 'Abel Jekyll. You also met my brother, Cain. This is our home, but it is also the only refuge for monsters hunted by the Chief Butler.'

'Pleased to meet you.' Mel wasn't the slightest bit pleased: his leg hurt, his arm howled with pain and he was sure half the skin off his back had been left on the stone flags thanks to being dragged here. He was more than halfway to hating the Jekylls. Why were they doing this to him?

'We have strict rules to maintain this sanctuary,' Abel said, answering Mel's question before he had a chance to ask. 'I was going to dispose of you out the back entrance but it seems my brother needed our particular strength just at that moment. I deduce that that means your protector is fighting for you. I'm not convinced even Cain and Viorica will be enough to deter that magnificent creature. You have clearly earned her loyalty. How did that happen?'

Mel could not think of any reason why he shouldn't tell the truth. 'I got her out of the ice where she had been frozen. She'd been there for sixty years.'

'Newton's apple!' Abel caressed his upper lip with a long forefinger, boyish enthusiasm warming his eyes. It made him look more like an ordinary fifteen-year-old, rather than the frighteningly mature person who had met them on the stairs. 'So it is possible to preserve life at sub-zero temperatures. I knew it!' He turned his back and started making rapid notes in a journal on the desk, like a pupil late to complete an essay assignment.

Mel knew his best chance was to delay until Eve found him again. He shuffled over to a low sofa and hauled himself up on to it. The softness was a blessing after the agonies of the last hour. The *scritch-scratch* of Abel's pen nib carried on, a comforting sound as it meant his captor was absorbed in his thoughts.

The door to the courtyard clapped open and Eve strode in. She looked battered, her clothes rent and her hair in a tangle, but she had clearly emerged undefeated.

'Mel Foster?'

'Here, Eve.'

She examined him with a sweep of her eyes, nodded then turned to Abel. 'You will give us shelter.'

'Of course, mademoiselle. *Mi casa es su casa*. Now tell me how you came to be in the ice?'

'You shelter Mel Foster too?'

'That is undecided.' He held his pen up over the creamy page of the journal. 'He is not a monster.'

'Neither are you!' protested Mel.

Abel gave him a sarcastic smile. 'Are you so sure of that?'

Eve wrinkled her uneven brow. 'What makes a monster?'

Abel leant back in the chair he was using, one that revolved on an ingenious mechanism that also allowed him to rock backwards. 'A good question.' He put down the pen and picked up a cricket ball from the desk, tossing it thoughtfully. 'I would suggest a certain excess of some quality above and beyond normal human capacity – for example, strength.' He gestured to her with a flourish of the ball. 'Also exaggeration or grossness in appearance adds to the overall effect.'

'Then I say Mel Foster is a monster.'

Abel snorted with laughter. 'What? That boy? You can meet a thousand like him in every corner of this city: street rats, guttersnipes, call them what you will.'

'*Non*, you are incorrect.'

Mel wiped a bead of sweat from his brow. It was a bizarre end to the day to hear Eve defend him in this philosophical discussion.

'How so, mademoiselle?'

'He has excess – an excess of kindness and loyalty.'

Abel smiled at her clever reasoning. 'And what of his appearance?'

'To me, he is grossly small.'

'Not to others. I won't allow that argument.' Abel spun the chair in a circle and bounced the ball off the wall, catching it neatly in cupped hands as he completed the turn.

Eve chewed on her lip. 'But you say there are thousands like him? Then he is exaggeratedly ordinary.'

'Bravo, but still a flimsy reason.'

'How about the fact that I'm on the Chief Butler's Wanted list?' said Mel.

'You are on his Monster List?' Abel tossed him the ball.

Mel fumbled the catch – he had a broken arm after all. 'I am.'

'Oh, this is good news!'

It sounded like terrible news to Mel.

'It means that we can let you in on a technicality without breaking our rules. The Chief Butler has put you on the Monster List, ergo, you are a monster.' Abel strode over to Mel and shook his hand. 'Welcome to the Monster Hideout, Master Foster.'

'Thank you.'

Abel scooped up the cricket ball and pressed it into Mel's palm. 'That's subject to our usual terms and conditions – and pending approval by all our members, naturally.'

'Naturally,' Mel said weakly, head whirling at the swift changes of Abel's mood.

Eve slumped down beside Mel, letting her exhaustion show at last. It had been a rough day for her, what with being struck by an artillery shell and numerous bullets, and then having to fight off a vampire and Abel's brother.

'So you will not attack Mel Foster again?' she asked.

'No, mademoiselle, and I will make sure the other monsters know he is not to be harmed.'

'Then I rest.' With that she folded her hands under her cheek and fell asleep.

'Extraordinary!' muttered Abel, examining her with a magnifying glass.

Mel rubbed his eyes, wanting to stay awake to defend Eve. A bat flew in through an open window. Having checked that Abel was in one piece, the vampire circled and hung upside down from the rafters. Even with Viorica roosting overhead, Mel finally had to give in to sleep. He nodded off to the whisper of Abel's pen on paper.

The cabinet was summoned to gather at midnight in the White Drawing Room of Buckingham Palace. Mr Copperfield took a couple of steadying breaths before entering with his shorthand notebook. The room was splendid with candles and candelabra, a crowd already gathered at the long table.

'So, Copperfield: you're here.' The Chief Butler sat at its head. He was dressed in an unbuttoned guardsman's uniform, bearskin helmet on the chair beside him. Mr Copperfield had an inkling that Burlington had known about every second he had spent in the corridor outside, gathering his courage to come in.

'Yes, sir.'

'Make sure you keep up with the discussion. I want a full transcript in triplicate by the morning.'

'Of course, sir.'

Mr Copperfield hurried over to a gilt and cream chair that stood against the wall, under a picture of a duchess dressed in a flouncy white gown. He noticed that someone had painted a moustache on to her upper lip and added horns to her forehead. Pad on his knee, pencil in hand, he waited.

Burlington called the cabinet to order.

'Welcome, ladies and gentlemen, to the second meeting of the Cabinet of Curiosities.' A hush fell in the chamber. The gathering of extraordinary people at the table made an alarming contrast to the white silk wallpaper and gilt plasterwork around them; a few looked insane and the rest murderous. 'First, allow me to introduce you to two new members. Lady Bracknell, already known to many of you,' he gestured to a fierce-looking woman decked in diamonds who was peering at her fellow government officials through a gold lorgnette. 'She has taken over at the Board of Trade.'

She stood up and stabbed a jewelled dagger into the briefing papers in front of her.

There was a smattering of applause from those gathered.

Mr Copperfield was taking all this down for the national archives. *Trade Secretary Bracknell demonstrated that she was on top of her brief.*

'Mrs Wessington, you are fading.' Burlington rapped on the table.

Mr Copperfield looked up and gulped. A ghostly woman dressed in the rags of a mid-century dress floated back to her seat. He had had to get used to such sights round the Palace of late. The monsters and other uncanny creatures that had been rounded up had been given a choice: either join Burlington or be caged. Mrs Wessington was one who had offered her services happily and been rewarded with a cabinet post.

'Apologies, Chief Butler.' Her voice was as thin as spiderwebs.

'Don't let it happen again or I will take away the Ministry of Transport from you. Your fleet of phantom rickshaws will be mothballed.'

Mrs Wessington wailed. 'Please no, Chief Butler!'

He pointed to her chair.

Once Mrs Wessington was put in her place, Burlington returned to introductions. 'The second member to join us is Mr Dorian Gray. I have put him in charge of the Queen's picture collection.'

A handsome man in a dapper suit, lily in his lapel, rose and bowed to the assembly. 'Charmed to join this illustrious cabinet.'

The members murmured their approval.

'Butler *sahib*, is the Queen not joining us tonight?' asked Foreign Secretary Gunga Dass, a shrewd looking Indian with a sweeping white moustache.

'Unfortunately, the Queen had been overset by some bad news. We were expecting delivery of a giantess from the Arctic, but the monster escaped and evaded capture. The disappointment has driven Her Majesty to her bed.' Burlington smiled, a glimpse of his black tongue sliding over his teeth.

'But to more serious matters: this giantess. She appears to be in the control of a human boy. Orders have been issued for his immediate arrest and incarceration . . .'

Mr Copperfield coughed.

'Yes, Copperfield?'

'Did sir misspeak? Do you not mean interrogation?'

Burlington held the private secretary's gaze. '*Incarceration*. I would like all of you to instruct your people to set his capture as their highest priority. He must be brought to me.' The ministers muttered to their neighbours. This was unprecedented.

Lady Bracknell raised a hand. 'Forgive me for asking, sir, but why this boy?'

'Because, madam, we cannot afford to have the rebellious wandering free in London, aiding loose monsters. He is a threat to the new, strong order we are introducing, where monsters either work with us or face the consequences.'

A collective shiver ran round the table with mutters of 'Quite so!' and 'Hear, hear!'

'Capture this child, Melchizedek Foster, in whatever way seems appropriate. I'll dispose of him myself.' Burlington gave the company a chilling smile.

Lady Bracknell dropped her lorgnette in surprise. 'But I know that boy! He was one of my orphans, a protégé of Dr Foster.' She shuddered. 'I had no idea you were talking about him. I could smell the happiness on him, so I sent him to sea. He should be dead.'

'You did what?' An ominous silence fell. 'I have been looking for this child for the past few months, Lady Bracknell, but you tell me now you sent him to sea! This is not an auspicious beginning to your cabinet career.' Burlington stood up and leant across the table with his weight resting on his knuckles, face a few inches from hers. 'How dare you?'

Lady Bracknell flinched at Burlington's harsh tone.

'Let me show you what happens to those that get in my way.' Burlington struck his fist on the table. The double doors at the far end of the room opened and unseen guards shoved a terrified gentleman inside. 'Mr Wallace, tell my cabinet what you did.'

Mr Wallace's forehead beaded with sweat as he stumbled to the foot of the table. His eyes darted left and right, looking for a way to escape. He had a pitchfork mark branded on his left cheek, the same sign that Burlington used to stamp official papers. 'I let the monster carry off the boy. I apologize once again, Your Excellency.'

'I do not forgive, Wallace. I have already told you that.' The Chief Butler threw a sheet of paper towards Lady Bracknell. 'Wallace has drawn up a description of the boy. Circulate it, capture the child, and perhaps your sorry part in this can be overlooked.' Burlington's eyes flicked to Lady Bracknell's face. He tapped a fingernail against his own cheek, threat plain. 'Start with this man that protected him – Dr Foster.'

'I'll see to it at once, sir.' The lady stood up, her complexion turning grey. 'If you'll excuse me.'

'Dismissed.'

She swept out, beckoning the unfortunate Wallace to follow her.

'That concludes our business.' Burlington dismissed the rest of the cabinet with a careless flick of his hand. They hurried out, Mrs Wessington hurrying *through* some of the ministers in her haste to flee his anger.

'What did you think of that?' Burlington asked, as the door closed behind the last minister.

'Me, sir?' squeaked Mr Copperfield.

'Yes, you.' Burlington turned in his chair and crossed his legs. Was that a bare foot peeking out of the bottom of his guardsman's trousers? The man had no sense of decorum! 'I keep you alive for your ordinary man's opinions. Tell me what you think.'

Mr Copperfield was more than ready to speak his mind but feared he was about to make an enormous mistake. 'I thought it a little harsh, sir, to pursue the boy.'

'A little?'

'Well, actually, a lot,' Mr Copperfield mumbled. 'Imprisonment without trial and whatnot.'

'Excellent!' Burlington got up and thumped his fists together. 'I was hoping you would say that. Type up these notes and leave them for the Queen and me to read in the morning.'

Mr Copperfield doubted that the monarch was in a fit state to read anything. No one had seen her for days. He was rather afraid she was dead, or imprisoned by this terrifying man. A little patriotic bravery reared its head.

'She is all right, the Queen, pray, sir?' he asked tentatively.

Burlington gave him a vicious smile. 'She's never been better, Copperfield. Never.'

Chapter Eight
Monsters Under the Bed

Mel's first day at the Monster Hideout revealed how little he had known about what was really going on in London. He had assumed that the city was peopled by, well, people. Now he discovered that many of those whom he had thought to be human were really other creatures in disguise. With the public on high alert and Monster Patrolmen on the streets, the ones who could no longer conceal their nature, or who had been found out, had taken refuge in the Jekylls' hideout.

The first two monsters he came across lived under his bed. He supposed he should have expected this, as it was a traditional hiding place, but he had been asleep when Eve had carried him to his chamber. He could be forgiven for not checking. It was the scuttling that alerted him to their presence. He opened his eyes, light falling diagonally across his bed from the chink in the curtains.

'Who's there?'

No reply, unless seeing his boot thrown across the room was a reply. He lay for a moment debating if he wanted to know what was underneath him.

He decided he did. He had faced a vampire – what could be worse? And it was daytime. Nothing too scary could be out now, surely? He propped himself up on his good elbow, then hung over the edge of the bed to look.

'Aaargh!' he cried.

'Eeek!' they screamed.

Flopping back on the pillow, Mel rubbed his eyes. He had come face-to-face with two of the ugliest fairies he had ever met. Not that he had met any real fairies before, but the ones in the picture books in shop windows were all beautiful, dressed in gossamer robes with long flowing hair. They certainly did not have faces that looked like knobbly potatoes, big pointy ears and scrubby brown hair. Or sharp teeth. He was sure he had spotted fearsome rows like a tiny shark's. As far as he could make out, the only part of the legend that was true were the pretty dresses.

Recovering from his shock, he tried again.

'Hello?' He lowered himself to look underneath the bed. 'Sorry about shouting just now. I'm Mel.'

The two fairies were cowering in the corner, arms around each other.

'I'm quite harmless.'

'But . . .' said one in a shaky voice, 'you've got your head on upside down!'

Mel decided that these two fairies would win no prizes for intelligence. 'No, I haven't. I'm just leaning over the edge of the bed to look at you. If you come out, you'll see I'm quite ordinary really.' He lay on his back waiting for them to find the courage to emerge.

With mutterings and thumpings, the two fairies clambered up to the footboard and sat on top of it to take a good look at him.

'He's right,' said the first, who was dressed in a floaty dress of pink silk that looked bizarre with his black boots and spiky beard.

'You sure?' The second one had his arms folded across his hairy chest, lemon gauze skirts not quite hiding his bony knees.

'He's just a boy. Boring!'

'Sorry,' muttered Mel, rather resentful that he wasn't enough to entertain them. 'Excuse me for asking, but you are fairies, aren't you?'

The bearded one picked his nose. 'Yeah. Monster fairies.'

Mel tried to puzzle that one out. 'What's the difference between you and the ordinary sort of fairy?'

'Same difference as between that giantess of yours and you, I'd say.' The monster fairy jumped on to the bed and stomped up the bedclothes to hold out a hand to Mel. 'I'm Nightmare, or Nightie.'

Mel shook the offered hand.

'I'm Inky – short for Incubus,' said the other, waving from the bedpost.

'Pleased to meet you, Inky. So you're living here, are you?'

'We're hiding from the humans.' Nightie sat cross-legged on the rainbow patchwork quilt. 'Girls, mostly. Can't find a decent hiding place at the bottom of the garden these days without some know-it-all chit with a camera trying to capture you for posterity.'

Inky blew a raspberry. 'You wanted to pose! It was your fault we got caught!'

'Yeah, well, how was I to know that the bloomin' Chief Butler would send one of his squads to collect us? It was only us being so ugly like that saved us. Our wigs came off and gave the Patrolmen the fright of their life.'

'You see, we're that dream you have when you're a nipper, when your pretty doll suddenly comes alive and develops teeth. Grrr!' Inky bared his fangs. 'It's not a bad job. Nice togs.'

'But that's all at an end now.' Nightie blew his nose on the hem of his pink gown with a noisy rasp. 'We've been outed, so we have to hide or end up at the Palace. The Jekylls have been top chaps letting us stay on their staff. We are the footmen here.'

'Who else is there?' asked Mel, wondering what

exactly he would encounter when he ventured from the room.

Nightie began counting off on his fingers. 'On the monster team there are the twins and that new vampire girl, but you've met her, they say.'

Mel nodded.

'Then there's the raven – he lives in the library, roosts on the bust of Athena over the natural history collection – he acts as messenger.'

'Don't forget the bottle imp. He's on a shelf in the pantry. Whatever you do, don't disturb him: he'll sell your soul to the Devil if you cross him.'

'What kind of bottle is he in?'

Inky shrugged. 'The normal kind. That's the catch.'

Mel made a note to avoid any kind of bottle in this house.

'Then there's us staff. The Egyptian mummy, he does most of the cooking and driving. And the butler, Mr Marley. '

'I'm not likely to meet anyone except you.' Mel gestured to his broken leg. 'I won't be going anywhere for a bit.

'Ah, but the Jekylls will have you fit in two shakes of a lamb's tail,' said Nightie. 'Good at human anatomy, they are.'

Mel remembered the dissecting table in the laboratory. 'I bet they are. Who exactly are they? Do they have any other family?'

Inky shook his head. 'Nah, they're on their own. Dad died a while back. They inherited his house and . . .'

Nightie elbowed him in the ribs. Inky shut his mouth.

'And what?' asked Mel.

'Nothing.' Inky began to whistle with unconvincing innocence.

'It was nice to meet you, Mel,' said Nightie, sliding off the cover to the floor. 'Must dash. Come along, Inky.'

'Toodle-pip!' Inky somersaulted off the bedknob. 'See you later, alligator!'

The two monster fairies scurried out in a flutter of silk and gauze.

Mel slumped back on his pillow, not quite sure what he made of them. He decided there could be worse monsters living under his bed.

Eve visited him shortly after the fairies' departure. She entered carrying a tray laden with breakfast – toast, butter, marmalade, bacon and eggs, pot of tea and milk, a little bottle made of blue cut glass, a pink rose in a long-stemmed vase. The food was set out on the finest crockery, decorated with gilt dandelion clocks.

'The fairy footmen said you wake up.' Eve put the tray down on his lap.

'Thank you.' Mel spotted a new ribbon in her hair – turquoise silk. The fairies' doing, he suspected.

She sat on the end of the bed, making the springs groan and the tea slop out of the spout, arms around her knees, feet on the covers. 'They look for you, Mel Foster.'

Mel chewed on his mouthful of toast and swallowed. His belly sighed with satisfaction. 'Inky and Nightie? But they know where I am.' The marmalade glistened, thick rinds emerging from the jelly like a pod of whales from the sea.

'Not them: the government. The Jekyll twins say that there are posters all over town that say "Most Wanted – little black-haired boy answering to the name Melchizedek". And they are offering a big reward for your capture.'

Such a pursuit seemed very far away while he was lying in bed eating a hearty breakfast. 'But why me and not you? I don't really qualify as a monster, only a technical one.'

'The twins don't know. You are the first human put on the list. They will send Viorica to see if she can find out why, but she prefers to do her work after dark.' Eve nudged the blue bottle towards him. 'The twins say Mel Foster must drink that. It will make bones mend.'

Remembering the fairies' warning about the bottle imp, Mel picked it up and studied it. 'Where did it come from?'

'Their laboratory.'

'Not the pantry?'

'No.'

He removed the cork. The liquid inside resembled

tar so thick he was able to pour it on to his toast. It now looked like dark-blue melted cheese.

'Are you sure this is a good idea?'

Eve shrugged. 'Abel said he hates lazy people. Everyone in the house is expected to work, not lie in bed.'

A cure offered for practical rather than compassionate reasons was easier to trust. 'Down the hatch, then.'

It tasted worse than it looked, like crushed sea slugs strained through old bandages. Mel quickly chased it down with a spoonful of marmalade. Immediately, his stomach grew hot and angry. 'Tea!' he croaked.

Eve poured him a cup, adding plenty of milk. Seeing his face, she put six sugar lumps in the drink and passed it to him. He gulped. No change: his belly still felt as though it was experiencing a volcanic eruption. 'Tray!'

Eve whisked it away, allowing Mel to bend over and cradle his middle.

'I think they're killing me!'

Eve looked anxious now. '*Non*, they would not dare! They know I will destroy this house if they harm a hair on your head!'

'It's more than a hair,' grunted Mel. His intestines writhed. The burning extended to his blood. His skin tingled, feeling on the point of splitting from his bones.

'Mel Foster, you are changing! Stop it!' Eve stood

up and pulled the covers off him. Mel could see that his thin legs were thickening, sprouting thick dark hairs, muscles bulging. His spine bowed, arms lengthened, bones popping out of sockets, growing and swelling.

'Help!' His voice was now a growl.

Eve ran to the door. 'Abel! Cain! *Venez-ici*!'

After a short pause, the twins sauntered in, elegant Abel in a stylish blue striped waistcoat and black trousers, rough Cain in a tweed jacket and baggy linen breeches. Abel checked his pocket watch.

'Please don't worry yourself, mademoiselle, everything is going to plan.'

What plan was that? Mel wanted to shriek. The plan where they killed him off in their bizarre experiment?

'Put up with the pain for the gain, boy,' said Cain sternly, taking Mel's pulse with an ungentle grip on his wrist.

'Your bedside . . . manner . . . is . . . somewhat lacking!' gasped Mel, curling up into a ball then throwing himself out like a starfish.

Abel grinned at his brother. 'I like this one. I'm glad we didn't have to throw him to the Chief Butler's dogs.'

Eve wrung her hands. 'But he is suffering! Help him!'

'Nah, he's mending.' Cain stole the last slice of toast off the tray and devoured it.

'Be not afraid, mademoiselle, no harm will come to him while he is in our sanctuary.' Abel closed his watch and tucked it back in his pocket. He patted Mel's shoulder. 'Almost there.'

The shrieking pain was receding, becoming a whimper. Mel sprawled, sweat running down his face. He wiped it off his cheek before anyone mistook it for tears.

'Mel Foster! Your left arm!' exclaimed Eve.

Mel had just used his broken arm to rub his face. His no longer broken arm. Amazed, he looked down at his toes. The swelling was going down and his legs were returning to their usual state. He lifted the right one, then the left. Apart from a dull ache, both were working perfectly.

'I really am healed!' He beamed at Eve, memory of the pain fast disappearing.

Abel moved to the door. 'Splendiferous, old bean. Now that's been sorted, we expect you in the library in half an hour. My brother and I are just going to change.'

'Do I have to?' growled Cain.

'Well, it is my turn, brother mine,' coaxed Abel.

The fairies cartwheeled into the bedroom as the twins departed.

'Don't forget: library meeting,' called Abel.

'All tickety-boo?' asked Nightie, jumping on the bed.

'Better than ever.' Mel displayed his mended arm to the inquisitive fairies. He regretted now that he had doubted the twins' good intentions. 'Excuse me, but I need to get up. Master Abel said to meet them in the library.'

Inky giggled. 'Abel? No, that was Cain. Wasn't it, Nightie?'

'Cain, Abel, Abel, Cain – never can tell betwixt the twain,' sang Nightie, zooming out of the room. Inky tripped over his skirts as he followed, leaving Mel and Eve scratching their heads in confusion.

Chapter Nine
Boy Hunt

Pausing on the threshold, Mel saw that he was not the only one summoned to the library. The raven perched on top of a bookshelf, brooding, head held low between two hunched black wings. Viorica lay on a sofa, completely still; she looked as if she was asleep, but did the undead sleep or just return to being dead? Eve waited by an armchair she had positioned in a warm spot for her friend. Cain and Abel sat in matching chairs behind the enormous desk, its surface clear apart from the dark-green leather and gilt-edged top, and an ink stand with a golden pen.

Mel had the distinct feeling this interview was more like a trial. He cleared his throat. 'I'm here.'

The rough twin pointed to the armchair with his hairy finger. Mel decided he would assume the elegant one was Abel and the rough one Cain until he heard differently. 'Park yourself there, mate.'

Mel looked up at Eve and raised his eyebrows to ask what was going on. She shook her head slightly, sharing his ignorance. Mel sat.

'The formalities first,' said Abel smoothly. 'My brother and I would like to put before you two new applicants for our protection: Eve Frankenstein, that unique young lady before you, and her friend, Melchizedek Foster, a boy.'

The raven squawked.

'Yes, indeed,' said Abel, addressing the raven, 'you're right: he is too ordinary for us under usual circumstances, but he's on the Monster List so we deem him an honorary member of our club.'

The bird fluttered its wings, then settled back to a grumpy silence.

'Lady Dracula, any objections?'

Languidly, the vampire sat up. 'I have but I believe you have made up your minds.'

'True. Your objections are noted. And I would also remind you that you were the one to bring them here, even though you are still in your probationary period as a resident in this house.'

Viorica glared at Abel.

'In that case, Mademoiselle Frankenstein, Melchizedek Foster, welcome to the Monster Hideout. Now, to business.' Abel rose, opened a satchel and spread a selection of advertising bills on the desk. 'The boy here – he's a puzzle. Why is Burlington after him and not the giantess? His name and description are on every billboard in London. The newspapers all carry Wanted notices for him. The reward has been raised to a thousand pounds.'

Viorica looked at Mel speculatively.

'A reward none of us will be claiming,' Abel said severely, fixing her with his gaze.

Cain growled. 'He's ours now.'

Viorica shrugged. 'So be it.'

'What is so special about Master Foster?' continued Abel. 'Granted, he is the friend of Miss Frankenstein, but she is hardly mentioned in connection to the boy-hunt. The Chief Butler sees this human as a threat – and that makes him very, very interesting.' Abel tapped his fingers together. 'Master Foster, do you have an explanation?'

Mel tugged at his collar. The twins had lent him a set of their old clothes: starched white linen and a superfine wool suit. He would have preferred something less expensive and more comfortable. 'No, I don't. I've not met this cove, this Chief Butler. I'm nobody.'

Abel toyed with his magnifying glass; Cain glowered as he sank deeper in his chair, scratching his muscular forearms.

'You can't be nobody,' grunted Cain. The tufts of hair sprouting from his ears twitched with impatience. 'You've got to be somebody. Who were your parents, eh?'

'I don't know, sir. All I know was that Dr Foster found my mother and me on the road to Gloucester soon after I had been born. It was such a terrible journey the doctor vowed never to go there again.'

'Dr Foster? Who's he?' asked Viorica.

'Do-gooder, known for his charitable works,' replied Abel. 'Lives on Gower Street. Odd you should mention him. Cain, have a read of that.' He passed the newspaper to his brother, pointing out a paragraph. 'Go on, Master Foster.'

'A thunderstorm brought on early labour. I'd only just been born when I was struck by lightning – at least that's what my mother claimed. The doctor thought that unlikely as he doubted I would've survived. Though I do have an odd scorch mark on my chest from the key that was around my neck.' Mel squeezed his hands in his pockets, embarrassed to have to account for himself before strangers. 'He took us to the poorhouse. My mother died soon after without revealing either the name of my father or her own.' Mel focused on the surface of the desk rather than look at the twins.

'Show us the mark, then,' said Cain.

Mel unbuttoned his shirt. The outline of the key had been burned into his skin. 'It matches the shape of the key exactly.'

Abel approached him with a magnifying glass. 'Curious.'

'The poorhouse wouldn't take a child born outside

the parish, so Dr Foster took me back to London to an institute he supports: Mr Wackford Squeers's Orphanage for Indigent Children.'

Viorica narrowed her eyes at the mark. 'And the key?'

'I think Dr Foster has that. It would've been stolen from me at the orphanage. The doctor came to visit me a few times a year and always on my birthday. He told me about the key when I turned eight.' The visits had been special days for Mel as his sponsor always gave him a whole bag of sugar mice as a present. He remembered the cool, creamy, minty taste even now, the way the sweets crumbled and melted on the tongue.

'Dr Foster has saved other children,' mused Abel, 'and I do not see a reward going up for their capture.' He turned to Mel. 'Unfortunately, the doctor has disappeared, so we cannot ask him what he knows.'

'Disappeared?' asked Mel fearfully.

'Yes. Just last night, on return from a visit to Lady Bracknell's house – it was in all the papers this morning – appeals for his safe return and so on. The theory is that he wandered out in that heavy shower and lost his way. The police think he might have been murdered in a backstreet, but his body hasn't been found. Perhaps a rogue monster got him? London is a dangerous place, even more so now that so many monsters are desperate.'

Mel shook his head. That didn't sound right: since the trip to Gloucester, Dr Foster was too afraid to wander about in the rain. The one birthday visit he had missed when Mel was nine had coincided with a downpour. He waited until the next day before calling.

Viorica spoke up. 'So, how are we to discover what Burlington sees in this boy?'

'Does it matter?' asked Eve, putting a hand on Mel's shoulder. 'We keep him hidden, the interest will pass and he will be safe.'

Abel came out from behind the desk to sit on the front edge. He folded his arms, head cocked arrogantly to one side. 'Of course it matters, mademoiselle. Until this point we have been fighting a losing battle against Burlington and the Monster Patrol.'

Surely Abel was overstating what they had achieved? thought Mel, looking around the room. 'Fighting? Is that what you've been doing? All I can see are creatures hiding behind closed doors as the Butler picks you off one by one.'

'Insolence!' Abel's green eyes glittered.

'Nah, he's right, Abel,' said Cain, wiping his nose on his sleeve. 'We've been on the back foot for months. We've got to move from providing a haven to taking action. It strikes me that if the Chief Butler is busting a blood vessel trying to capture Mel then the boy could be his weakness. We must find out why that is.'

'Of course, he might just not like the child,' said Viorica. 'I cannot say that I am too fond of him myself.'

Mel was tempted to make a rude sign at her. All he had done was refuse to be her dinner.

Cain shook his head. 'Burlington doesn't like anyone. This is different –'

'Promising,' added Abel.

'I'm pleased now we didn't throw you out, mate.'

'And we will keep you here at least until the mystery is solved.'

'Thank you.' Mel thought the twins could be making too much of a few Wanted posters. He knew he was nothing special: just a common-or-garden orphan who happened to get himself mixed up with monsters.

'So, we have a new task. Get ourselves organized and find out why Burlington is putting so much effort into tracking the boy.' Abel gestured to the door, a sign of dismissal.

Viorica glided out, followed by the raven. The twins looked as if they considered the meeting concluded, but Mel still had many unanswered questions. His life so far had taught him that there was no such thing as free board and lodging. 'Please, Master Jekyll, can you explain what you would like me to do while I'm here? I'm not bad at polishing and cleaning. I know how to tie knots and climb rigging, not that there's much call for that round here.'

The twins exchanged a long look. It was almost as if they could speak mind to mind.

'Agreed,' said Cain.

Abel picked a strand of dark hair off his lapel. 'Master Foster, we would like to run a few simple experiments on you to ascertain your particular qualities.'

'Experiments?' asked Mel warily. He remembered the mending medicine queasily.

'Nothing that will harm you, we promise. And while you are acting as our subject, you duties will be light. A little dusting of the laboratory, nothing more. A third footman.'

Mel glanced up at Eve. She nodded. 'Do not worry, Mel Foster. I will join the twins' Monster Resistance. I also have agreed to be examined. These young scientists are very curious about anything unexplained.'

Abel gave one of his cold smiles. 'Indeed, in your different ways you and the boy both represent puzzles in need of solving.'

Cain gave a rumbling laugh and belched.

Mel felt too unsure of his hosts to ask what kind of puzzle they were themselves. The way they seemed to exchange names on a whim was perplexing. One twin had been given all the sophistication, the other all the coarseness, yet they got on splendidly.

They were probably mad.

Then again, as they were the only ones showing any sign of standing up to the Chief Butler, maybe they were the only sane people left in London?

Mel dusted the skeleton in the corner of the laboratory, enjoying having the place to himself. Unlike the elegant house, the workroom was a practical brick annex, no fancy plasterwork or fine carpets. The twins and Viorica were away ferreting out information about Burlington's plans, the vampire using her bat form to eavesdrop, the twins to mingle with society rich and poor. No use on undercover missions, Eve had decided to venture into the kitchen to talk to the mysterious mummy cook about his tendency to spice things too highly.

The Jekylls' workroom was a fascinating place: books on the most modern advances in science sat alongside ancient treatises on alchemy and divination. Their equipment showed an equal mix of rational new and magical old. There was a yellow cylinder in a wooden frame attached to a contraption that sat on the head, covering the ears. When Mel put it on, he could hear a hiss and the sound of distant voices – very spooky. Spotless glass flasks and fleshy pink rubber tubes snaked from a copper still, a blue liquid dripping drop by slow drop into a collecting bottle. He recognized it as the mixture that had cured him, but had no desire to taste it again. Next to the still was a chest full of odds and ends of the fortune-teller's craft: glass ball, sparkly cloth, a pack of picture cards, dice with runes rather than numbers.

On the desk lay the journal in which Mel had seen Abel write his notes. He was still curious about the twins: in what way did they consider themselves monsters? Checking no one was near, he sneaked a look inside, ignoring the twinge of guilt. Two hands were evident. Both were beautifully neat, but one sloped to the left and the other to the right. The twins' interests were varied: notes on the pattern of the constellations in each month, the possibilities of the horseless carriage, something called crystal radio, improvements for what they termed the machine gun, a new attachment for a sewing machine, an alternative arrangement for a typewriter keyboard, and the potential for freezing life and reanimating it – this last inspired by Eve. The very last entry was short: just Mel's own name and a question mark.

The handle on the door to the laboratory dipped. Mel shut the book with a bang. The monster fairies tumbled into the room, Inky jumping off Nightie's shoulders where he had climbed to reach the knob.

'Here he is: the man of the moment!' declared Inky.

'*Boy* of the moment,' corrected Nightie.

'You've created turmoil out there, you have.' Inky jerked his thumb over his shoulder in the general direction of the streets. 'Worse than when the were-elephants escaped from London Zoo.'

'Were-elephants?' marvelled Mel.

'Amazing creatures – imported from India by the Foreign Minister,' explained Nightie. 'Like werewolves but the men turn into . . .'

'Elephants,' concluded Inky. 'Now, for you, there are checkpoints on every bloomin' corner. Few places for an honest . . .'

'Or a dishonest . . .' slipped in Nightie.

'. . . fairy to hide.'

Mel scratched his head. 'You're serious?'

Inky nodded. 'One hundred percent, my old cocklewasher.'

'But that's ridiculous.' Mel sat on the old sofa, cross-legged. The two fairies perched on the arm next to him.

'Want a sugar mouse?' Inky produced a battered paper bag from under his skirt. One mouse remained among the icing sugar.

'Thanks.' It looked a bit old, but Mel wasn't going to pass up a chance to taste his favourite sweet. It tasted exactly like the ones Dr Foster used to bring him. 'Where did you buy it?'

'Didn't buy it – confiscated it. It's evidence,' said Inky proudly.

Mel gave an awkward swallow. 'But I've just eaten it.'

Nightie hit Inky in the chest, pushing him off the sofa. 'You twit. We were going to show the scary twins!'

'What kind of evidence was it?' asked Mel.

Inky clambered back on to the sofa arm. 'We went snooping at your old patron's house. Dr Foster. He had a bag of these in his desk.'

'We ate the others,' added Nightie.

Inky peered inside the empty bag. 'He had a note on it, "For Melchizedek", but I think I've lost that.'

They really were the most hopeless detectives.

'He used to bring me these when he visited. Was

there anything else about me in his desk?'

'Nah. The place had been turned over before we came.' Nightie picked his teeth with the sharp end of a map compass. 'These were the only things left.'

'But that's really important! You have to tell the twins.'

'Tell us what?' Cain entered from the passageway leading to the back door. He hung his battered hat on a peg.

'Dr Foster's papers about me have been stolen.'

'Not unexpected. That was what we were going to do; just means someone else got there first.' Cain threw a sack on the dissection table. It writhed as if full of snakes. 'Scat, all of you: I've work to do. Go clean the stables.'

Mel trailed out after the fairies. They scuttled off to get back to their duties. Deciding cleaning a stable did not equal a 'light' task suited to a recently mended limb, Mel headed for the kitchen. As he approached he could hear Eve's voice raised, talking in rapid-fire French. He peeked in. Eve and the mummy stood either side of the stove like duellists about to fight. The mummy held a ladle raised over a bubbling pot, brown bandages trailing, a white apron fastened over his front. Attached to his neck was a label: Lot 248. It dangled like a necktie, threatening to dip into the soup. No features were visible on his face apart from a slight bump where his nose would be. Eve seemed to be arguing with the mummy in a mixture of French and sign language about the correct way to season vegetable ragout. It did not seem wise to interrupt.

Mel wandered off to the library and sat looking out over the street. Staying indoors waiting for the others to sort out his problems was frustrating. He was used to being on the move and looking after himself. He lifted the net curtain to peek out. People hurried by: quick-stepping maids carrying baskets, slouching apprentices with thumbs stuck in pockets, visitors to London with their Bradshaw railway timetables. Two Patrolmen strode purposefully down the centre of the pavement, a red menace forcing others out of their path. They stopped everyone, male and female, who was about Mel's height, removing the bonnet from one startled scullery maid and comparing a crossing sweeper with a description they had in their hands before letting him go back to work.

So the hunt was real.

Fear took a bite at Mel's heart. The oddity of his hiding place had distracted him from the truth. He was in more trouble than he had ever been in his entire life. The country he had thought he knew had turned during his months at sea into a foreign land in which he was not welcome. He wanted answers now even more than the twins. It was as though he had been charged with a crime he had no memory of committing. He would have to do something – write down everything he could remember – see if any hints lay in his past. That was better than sitting here waiting.

Then, just as he was about to drop the curtain, he caught sight of a familiar figure. Dr Foster was strolling down the pavement on the far side of the street with sharp efficient movements, rolled black umbrella used as a walking stick. He looked exactly like he did in the portrait of him at the orphanage, even down to the old-fashioned coat and pinstriped trousers.

'Eve!' Then Mel remembered she was in deep dispute with the mummy. 'Someone, please come!'

A ghost materialized beside Mel, making him jump. The gentleman had a handkerchief that attached his jaw to the rest of his head. A huge chain coiled around him like a boa constrictor, weighed down with cash boxes and keys. 'May I help you, young sir?'

'Who are you?' gulped Mel.

'The butler, sir.'

Mel tried to grab the sleeve of the butler's jacket but his hand passed straight through. 'Look, Mr Ghost, it's Dr Foster! Please go and ask him to come in!'

'My name is Marley, Jacob Marley.' The ghost mournfully shook his head. 'But I cannot roam during the daylight hours. I am doomed to haunt this town only in darkness, lamenting, moaning, sighing over my manifold –'

Mel cut him short. 'Yes, I understand, but this is an emergency!'

Out on the street, the doctor had passed the house and reached the corner. The impulse to catch him burned like dragon fire in Mel's belly.

'It cannot be done.'

'Then I'll have to go myself.' Mel headed for the door. Obeying rules had never been his strong point.

The ghost kept up with him, trying to block his path, but as he was insubstantial his efforts were futile. 'Please, young sir, that is most unwise. Your orders are to stay here out of sight.'

'But the man with the answers is out there.' Mel ran down the stairs, tripping in his haste. 'We've got this one chance. I can't let it pass.' He calculated that he had a few minutes before the Patrol circled back to this street on their beat. He could risk it.

Throwing the door open, Mel jumped down the front steps and raced up the street, dodging chimney sweeps and delivery boys, knife sharpeners and dairymaids. He felt marvellous, full of energy. His legs had never felt this strong. Whatever was in that blue medicine had worked wonders. Turning the corner into Russell Square, he caught sight of his quarry. Dr Foster was heading north.

'Dr Foster! Sir!' Mel darted across the street, dicing with death as he dodged between a hansom cab and a brewer's cart.

The doctor could not hear him over the clatter of hooves on cobbles but Mel was confident he would overtake him before he left the square. He hurdled a bookstall and slipped past a flower seller.

'Gotcha!' A hand hooked Mel's collar, bringing him to a sudden choking halt. If it had been his old ragged shirt, he could have ripped free, but the Jekylls' fine linen held firm. 'Where have you been, you dirty little orphan?'

Mel recognized that voice. He struggled as hard as he could to get loose but a blow to the back of his head stunned him.

'Stop that. Answer me.'

Mel could not plead mistaken identity, for the man who held him knew him very well indeed. He may have been a fool for going out but he was not a betrayer. Mel said nothing.

Mr Wackford Squeers, Jr, the director of the orphanage where Mel grew up, whistled. A hansom cab drew up alongside them.

'All right, guv, where to?' asked the cab driver.

'Bracknell Place, Park Lane. There's a big tip in this if you get us there in record time.'

'Righto, gov.' The cab driver touched his narrow-brimmed hat with his whip.

'In you get.' Squeers shoved Mel into the cab. Mel tried to scramble back out, but the orphanage director prevented this by sitting on him. The cab surged into motion. Squeers gave a chuckle. 'What a piece of luck! We've all been looking for you, and here you fall right into my hands! What were you doing in this part of town, boy?'

Mel stared stubbornly at the cracked-leather door lining.

'Not going to tell me?' Squeers cackled, amused by Mel's defiance. 'I don't suppose that matters. Lady Bracknell has plenty of questions for you, and I must say, her methods of extracting answers are very effective.' Squeers took a packet of liquorice out of his pocket and chose a lozenge. The chewing noise he made turned Mel's stomach. Squeers's weak chin moved up and down, rusty sideburns circulating like pistons. His skin had always been blotched and flaky, and little scales of dandruff rained on Mel. The orphanage director smacked his lips. 'Thank my lucky stars I had a meeting in this part of town this morning. I wasn't even looking for you just then. But some things are meant to be, eh?'

Chapter Ten
A Model Major General

'An express has arrived from Lady Bracknell, sir.' Mr Copperfield waited outside the Chief Butler's private quarters, which were in the chamber formerly called the music room. Now the only sounds that came from there were the shrieks and howls of the monster captives Burlington interrogated, none of them tuneful. Only last week, on refusing to join him, several ghosts had been exorcised and a family of were-bears defanged and sent to the Zoo.

The door opened, releasing the smell of burning rubber. Mr Copperfield ventured in, heart throbbing in his throat.

The heavy drapes were pulled across the window. Burlington was reclining on a divan in a red-satin dressing gown. A dark-eyed girl with a long flowing dress in the style of the previous century sat combing his hair while another pretty lady in a lace cap polished his sharp toenails. A huge fire leapt in the grate, even though it was a warm day. Sweat ran down Mr Copperfield's back in the infernal heat.

'It is good news, I trust?' asked the Chief Butler.

'I would not presume to read your private correspondence, sir.'

'Why not? You are a *private* secretary.'

To the Queen, not to you, Mr Copperfield thought with a spurt of defiance. He masked it under a show of obedience. 'In future, with your permission, I will open all letters, sir.' He broke the seal on the message from Lady Bracknell. Placing his spectacles on his nose, he read: 'The lady writes that she has good news. She has . . . apprehended the boy and is holding him, awaiting your pleasure. Oh.' Mr Copperfield had been taking secret comfort from the fact that Mel Foster was evading capture.

'Excellent.' Burlington waved the girls away. They glided to the far wall where in the half-light they seemed to merge with a painting, a jovial scene of many young people gathered for a picnic in a vaguely Italian setting. Mr Copperfield blinked. Of course they could not climb into a picture; it had to be a hidden door. 'Order my carriage to be brought round, Copperfield. I will see to this matter personally.'

'Very good, sir.' Mr Copperfield backed out of

the room. He paused on the threshold. 'Oh, and sir, how is the Queen today, if I may be so bold as to enquire?'

'Resting.' The Chief Butler shrugged on a white Albanian silk coat and topped off his outlandish outfit with a gold turban.

'Then she is in good health?'

'Resting peacefully. Very peacefully. I suggest you offer the British public what reassurance they need that all is well.' Burlington dismissed Mr Copperfield with a flick of his fingers.

Mr Copperfield hurried away. Reassuring the public was one thing, but who was going to reassure him? It was his duty to see to the Queen's well-being. He was really going to have to do something about Her Majesty or lose all self-respect.

On his way to the coach house, the private secretary almost tripped over one of the Queen's disconsolate Pomeranians. The Chief Butler detested dogs, so they had been banished to the courtyard. The Pomeranian's wounded gaze reminded Mr Copperfield of the other person about whom he was worrying: the child, Foster, now in the hands of Burlington's cruellest minister. He would have to do something for that boy – if it fell within his power.

Oh dear, oh dear: so much he should do and so little chance he could help. Mr Copperfield felt extraordinarily disappointed in himself.

'Come along with you, Moppet,' Mr Copperfield told the dog. 'You're best off out of his way, you know.'

Lady Bracknell and Mr Squeers sat either side of the fireplace at Bracknell Place, her in a throne of red damask, he in a humbler armchair. On the carpet between them knelt Mel Foster, shivering. He was trying to think positive thoughts, but that strategy was failing. Mostly he was furious at himself for taking such a stupid risk.

The two adults were drinking tea, ripping hearty bites out of buttered muffins and crumbling slices of Victoria sponge that oozed thick strawberry jam. Mel had been offered nothing except a cuff for trying to run for it and a pistol brandished in his face as a warning against escape. At the moment it was prevented by the guard on the door: a young major general in a scarlet military jacket and white curled wig. Mel's eyes kept returning to him. There was something odd about the soldier, quite apart from the eighteenth-century cut of his coat and ancient wig. His expression never altered, but stayed fixed like he had been caught pulling faces when the wind changed.

Mel contemplated escaping up the chimney, but he guessed he had probably outgrown the role of sweep. Getting stuck somewhere his enemies could light a fire under him was a bloodcurdling thought.

Smug with success, Lady Bracknell and Mr Squeers

were discussing Mel's fate even though he was listening, so confident were they that Mel would not be able to tell anyone. He would soon be in the Butler's clutches.

'Lady Bracknell, the boy's capture will send you into the first rank of the Chief Butler's favourites,' said Mr Squeers, butter dripping from his chin. The lady's steel gaze speared the offending spot, and Squeers quickly dabbed the smear with a snowy napkin. 'A piece of luck, what?'

'Indeed, Mr Squeers, I will not forget the service you have rendered.' Her tone was far from grateful, coming in icicle stabs of words.

'Thank you, my lady.'

She poured herself a fresh cup of tea from the silver pot. 'I was considering your reward.'

Squeers's eyes lit up like a bulldog sensing dinner about to be served.

'A generous donation to your orphanage to be used at your discretion.' She patted the black beaded handbag on her lap. 'And I will take a few more of the brats off your hands. The Chief Butler has need of healthy young specimens. Now that nearly all the monsters have been rounded up, he is turning his attention to controlling the population.'

Squeers's Adam's apple bobbed as he swallowed. 'I'm not sure how many healthy ones I can provide.'

'Feed them up first. A week or two of a meat-and-potato diet and they should be strong enough. Send them to Wallace's studio at the National Gallery to have their photograph taken, and then to me.'

'Photographs?'

'Oh yes, we need a record of the little blighters.' Lady Bracknell spread butter on another muffin. 'Wallace knows what to do.'

Mel didn't like the sound of that for his fellow orphans, but he had his own more immediate fate to consider. He studied his hands, checking his lifeline on the left. Had it got shorter since last he looked?

A tapping on the window caught everyone's attention.

'Confounded bird!' Lady Bracknell turned her disapproving eye on a raven hopping along the broad grey sill.

'I'll get rid of it for you, ma'am,' said Squeers obsequiously. He crossed the room and threw up the sash. 'Get away! Shoo!'

The raven croaked and flapped into the air. Mel was no expert on the species, but it looked exactly like the one who lived in the Jekylls' library. He felt a glimmer of hope.

Squeers lowered the window and resumed his seat. 'What is it about this boy that has caught the Chief Butler's attention, my lady?'

Lady Bracknell added a nip of brandy to her tea. 'Our esteemed leader is adamant he has to be captured but I do not know the specific reason. He only mentioned that he has been seeking the child. What do your records say about him?'

'That his father was unknown. Mother a well-brought-up girl fallen on hard times. The child has a burn mark here.' Squeers pointed to his chest. 'Dr Foster was the only one who knew more.'

Lady Bracknell smiled, little finger crooked as she tipped her cup. 'Ah, yes: the good doctor. He was one of the first Burlington picked.'

Mr Squeers put down his cup, slopping the tea over the rim. 'One of the first what?'

'Recruits. For Mr Burlington's army. He had first to remove the threat from the monsters as they were the only ones with any real hope of defeating him, but now he's finished capturing all but the last few, he's moving on to quelling resistance from the general public.'

Mel hugged his knees. The doctor joining up with the Chief Butler? That was unlikely. He was a decent man.

'I can't see the old gent fighting,' said Squeers. 'He's always good for an extra guinea or two, but not anything involving action – too squeamish, too principled, too afraid of getting wet.'

Lady Bracknell sniffed in disdain. 'You do not understand, Squeers, the brilliance of our master's plan. It is not the man he needed but his image – as Dr Foster found out last night.'

'What? I mean, I beg your pardon?'

'The answer to that is on a strict need-to-know

basis. Only those closest to the Chief Butler have access to his plans for taking over the British Empire.' The sagging flaps of skin under Lady Bracknell's chin quivered like a turkey's wattle. 'I am in that number; you are not.'

'Naturally not, my lady,' said Mr Squeers bitterly. 'I just found your boy for you. I don't deserve to know anything, even though I have done what so many others failed to do.'

'Careful, Squeers, your ambition is showing.'

The clatter of hooves on the road outside broke up the brewing argument. Squeers put down his cup and hurried to the window.

'Is it him?' asked Lady Bracknell, getting up and smoothing her skirts nervously.

'Indeed, I believe so.' Squeers slicked back his drab brown hair and slapped some colour into his cheeks. As an afterthought, he kicked Mel. 'Stand up, boy. Show the Chief Butler some respect.'

Mel stood, trying to hide that he was shaking.

A shriek came from the floor below, then a wolf's howl and a crash. Something large and, from the sounds of it, very expensive had just been destroyed.

'What in Hades . . .!' exclaimed Lady Bracknell.

The maids were screaming.

'The Chief Butler must not see my house in uproar.' She snapped her fingers at the orphanage director. 'Squeers, delay the entry of the Chief Butler while I deal with this.' Squeers ran for the stairs. 'Major Anson, guard the boy!'

The soldier saluted. Lady Bracknell swept out.

Now was Mel's chance. With only one guard watching him, the odds of escape could not get better. He bolted for the door.

The major general drew his sword with a flourish, silver tip pointed at Mel's throat.

Mel grabbed a satin cushion from the sofa and threw it at the blade. General Anson sliced it away, leaving himself briefly open to attack. Mel charged, head lowered, aiming for the officer's midriff. As his head made contact, the soldier exploded in a shower of dry flakes. Mel's speed was so great he almost knocked himself out as he collided with the wall. He sprawled, stunned, on the carpet for a moment, bits of scarlet and gold raining on him.

Well, that certainly wasn't what he had expected.

The guard had not been real; he had been only a model, a marvellous creation of mechanical or magical genius.

No time to work it out. Mel got up, rubbing the bump on his forehead. He had to get away.

Running to the first floor balustrade, he took a quick look over. In the foyer, a wolf was battling two huge footmen who looked more like trolls than people. The Jekyll twins stood back-to-back, fighting off their attackers – six members of staff summoned from garden and stable. Abel brandished a pistol in one hand, a sword in the other; Cain favoured a club.

Cain caught sight of Mel. 'Garden gate – now!' he roared.

Taking that as an order to get away before the Chief Butler arrived, Mel ran for the far end of the first floor, through a darkened drawing room. A house like this always had a servants' staircase, usually hidden and inconvenient but at the moment just what Mel needed. He found the entrance beside a strange picture. The frame must once have held a portrait of a man, as his outline was still visible against the battlefield vista and fluttering flags. But someone had gone to the trouble of cutting out the figure. The model major general popped up in Mel's brain, but he had no time to fathom the connection. He tucked it away for later.

Opening the door, Mel listened. No one was moving on this stair; the commotion was all at the front of the house. He headed down, breath coming in shallow bursts. He stopped, undecided, when he reached the ground floor. He guessed that the only way out on this level was the grand front door; servants came and went by their own side entrance in the basement. He risked going down another storey to the cellars. Two doors led off from the foot of the stairs. Putting his ear to the one on the right he could hear the hubbub of a busy kitchen; to the left it was quiet. He would try that way first before braving the servants.

Decision made, Mel opened the door on the left. It led into the wine cellar. There was a dim light coming from a high, barred window that flickered as shadows of people and carriages passed on the street. That world seemed very far away in this sepulchral place. The air was damp and smelt of old vintages, a hint of the warm south, places he had visited in his voyages. Mel made his way along the racks. At the end was another door, bolted on this side. Hoping it was the way out he slid back the lock and eased it open.

What was this? Dr Foster lay on a narrow shelf, hands folded on his chest, eyes closed. He looked even older than Mel remembered, not at all like the brisk, dapper man he had spotted only hours ago. He did not appear to be breathing.

Alarmed, Mel crossed to him and felt for a pulse, remembering with a sense of deja vu the last creature on a wooden shelf he had touched. The same flick of energy sprang between him and Dr Foster. Then the doctor took a shuddering gasp of breath, chest heaving in frantic pants.

'It is all right, doctor. It's just me – just Mel.' Mel backed away. He didn't like this, not one bit. The doctor looked so frail and white, worn at the edges.

'Melchizedek?' The doctor's voice was paper-thin. 'Is that you?'

'Yes, sir.'

Some life flowed back into the old gentleman. He

turned his head, eyes wild. 'You have to escape, boy! They mustn't find you!'

That answered the question as to which side the doctor was on. 'I will, sir, but you're coming with me. You can't stay here.' He tugged the doctor's hand. 'Please, I'll help you.'

Dr Foster swung his legs over the edge of the shelf. Chips of what looked like paint rained from his black coat. 'I can't. There's something wrong with me.' He felt his face, tracing white whiskers and new lines. 'I've aged a decade. I have no strength left.' He looked in horror at his hands. 'I'm dissolving.'

Mel followed the direction of the doctor's gaze. His palms were flaking but where the gaps appeared was a substance like raw canvas, not flesh. Was the doctor another model like the soldier? But his face was different, showing all the emotions he was experiencing. Dr Foster seemed human in a way the guard had not.

'Please, we must get you out of here. I've friends – clever friends – they'll know how to fix you, but we have to get out first.' Mel put an arm around the doctor and heaved him to his feet.

'Escape. Yes, escape.' Dr Foster shuffled forward a step, moving warily as if expecting his legs to snap beneath his weight.

'Do you know this house, sir? Is there a way out the back to the garden gate?'

'Where are we?' The doctor scanned the wine racks

for clues. 'I have no memory of how I came to be here.'

'Lady Bracknell's house.'

A glint appeared in the doctor's eye. 'Still here, am I? I've been wandering in such dark dreams, I had no idea. Yes, yes, I am familiar with Bracknell Place. There is a back gate leading to Park Street. That way.'

They hobbled to the back door that opened on to the garden. Making their way past the lawn roller, they used the shrubbery to hide their progress along the path.

'What's all the noise?' asked Dr Foster, turning his head and dislodging another flake from his hair.

'I think you'd better not move too much, sir,' said Mel.

'I think you're right, boy. Very odd. Very odd indeed.' His hand shook as he studied it. He was trying to be brave for Mel's sake, but he was clearly deeply afraid.

'The noise is from the diversion to help us get away.' Mel hurried the doctor up the garden path. 'But we must hurry – our escape will soon be discovered.'

'I agree, my boy. I always knew you were a lad of exceptional intelligence.'

Not so bright, actually, thought Mel a moment later. He had not anticipated that the gate would be locked. He could climb over, but there was no chance that the doctor would be able do the same.

The raven flew past and cawed.

'Hang on, sir: I think help will be here soon.'

Dr Foster sagged against Mel and rubbed his heart. 'I really do feel very peculiar.'

Two hands took hold of the iron struts of the gate and yanked it from its hinges.

'Hello, Mel Foster. You are very much in trouble.' Eve grinned at him through black gauze. She wore a bonnet with a heavy veil, but no other girl in London had her height or strength. Mel had no doubt it was her.

'Eve, can you carry the doctor? Careful: he's very fragile.'

'*Bien sûr.*' Eve gently scooped Dr Foster up in her arms. His clothes left a dark smear on her skin. The doctor's head lolled back; he had lost consciousness again. 'He weighs very little and his smell is very peculiar. What is wrong with him?'

Mel followed her out on to Park Street where a carriage was waiting. He recognized the driver as the mummy, a coat and a tricorn hat over his bandages. Mel briefly wondered how the creature could see, but he was too eager to get away from Bracknell Place to worry. He got in after Eve and the horses clip-clopped down the street at a smart pace.

'I don't know what's wrong with the doctor,' Mel said, finding it difficult to speak, 'but I'm hoping the twins will have answers. If they don't, I fear we'll lose him for good.'

Chapter Eleven
Still Life

Anxiety over Dr Foster's condition distracted Mel from thinking about what he had done. Once he had seen the doctor safely placed in a bed in the room next to his own, the realization that he had let down his protectors came back with full force. The twins were not going to be happy that he had gone out despite numerous warnings that he was being hunted. Had they escaped unhurt? Mel wouldn't forgive himself if the others had suffered to save him.

'I'd best face the music,' he said under his breath.

Eve heard his mutter and patted his shoulder comfortingly, though her strength made his teeth rattle and would probably leave bruises. 'Don't worry, Mel Foster. Your doctor will receive the best care. These Jekyll twins are very clever.'

She was right: the real concern here was the wellbeing of the doctor, not what the Monster Resistance would do to Mel for disobeying orders. 'Do you know where they are?'

'They were to retreat when the raven alerted them that you were free. They should be back any moment.'

The crash of the front door being thrown back on its hinges announced their arrival.

'Mummy, put the carriage in the stables! Where is that confounded boy?' bawled one of the Jekylls.

Heavy feet pounded up the stairs. Mel braced himself for the coming storm.

'There you are!' Both brothers appeared on the landing, Viorica hovering at their backs. Her hair was still matted and grey, in the last stage of transition back from wolf, her nose shrinking from whiskery snout. Something odd was also happening to the Jekylls. In his fury, Abel's features blurred, becoming for a second more like his brother. Cain's face was doing the same, but in reverse.

Cain shoved his brother. 'Keep your hair on, Abel. You'll trigger a change if you carry on in this fashion.'

'I want to wring his stupid little neck!' Abel flexed his fingers, which were growing thicker by the second.

'Quite so.' Cain was sounding more elegant with every second. 'But it's my turn in this shape today.'

Abel took a deep, calming breath. His skin paled and smoothed and his hair took on a luxuriant curl, facial features chiselled rather than hacked. He puffed out a breath, reaching for his control. 'I apologize, Cain.'

His brother snorted. 'Just watch that temper of yours.' He winked at Mel. 'See, I'm the good-natured twin; he's the one you've got to worry about.'

So that was their secret! It wasn't names they had been exchanging but bodies.

'How . . .?' Mel began.

'Don't worry about that now,' snapped Abel, 'worry instead that you almost brought disaster on yourself and those that gave you sanctuary.'

Mel couldn't meet their eyes, finding the guilt too much. 'I didn't tell them where to find you, I promise. Are you all right?'

'Fortunately, yes. You're lucky we got out before we had to fight off the Chief Butler and his guards. If we'd still been there when he came inside, then it would have been a different story.'

'I'm sorry.' Mel felt it wasn't enough, but what else could he say?

'We believe you are – or we would have left you there to rot and moved to a new location.'

Cain gave a sceptical snort.

Abel flicked his brother a quelling look. 'But what possessed you to go out when you knew all of London was hunting for you?'

Mel knew his defence was weak. 'It was Dr Foster – at least, I thought I saw someone very like him in the street. But I found the real doctor at Lady Bracknell's, imprisoned in the cellar. I rescued him. He's in there now.' He gestured to the bedroom.

'What? Another human in our sanctuary? This is too much!' Abel shook his head in disgust. 'Cain, he can't stay here. You, Master Foster, will be the ruin of us.'

Mel gulped. 'You'll understand why I had to bring him when you see him. Please, you've got to help him. He's changed. I don't think he's quite human any more.'

Cain clumped over to the door. 'Let's at least see what he's found, Abel, before we throw him out. We did want to talk to the doctor, remember?'

With a muttered curse, Abel joined his brother and entered the chamber.

Viorica twirled on the spot like a child receiving an unexpected gift. 'You are in serious trouble, Mel Foster, for breaking the rules of the sanctuary. Soon you will be out on the streets, unprotected.' She tapped her cheek, pearly teeth visible as they pressed against her lower lip. 'Are you sure you won't give me just a little of your blood and win my support? I'm feeling hungry again.'

'He has my support, vampire, and always will,' Eve said stoutly, pushing Mel behind her. 'That is more than enough. The mummy has ordered some blood for you from Smithfield Market. Go drink that.'

Viorica wrinkled her nose. 'Pah! Ox blood – and a few hours old. I hate that stuff.' She ran her fingers through her grey wolf-locks, combing them out until they resumed their usual blonde silkiness.

'Why do you dislike me so much, Lady Dracula?' Mel had not thought he had earned this extreme hostility.

Her eyes flickered with red flame. 'Because I thought I was finally safe when I arrived here among the other monsters, no desire to bite anyone, no human blood pulsing in necks or scent of blood filling the corridors – safe, until you came. You've ruined everything. You're like a constant ache in my gut.'

'I can't help being human.'

'Master Foster, would you come in here please?' Abel no longer sounded angry – he had regained his usual politeness.

Mel arched a brow at Viorica. 'Looks like I'm no longer in his bad books.'

Viorica frowned, eyes flicking to the bedroom door. 'Perhaps I can drink from the doctor instead?'

Mel's alarm flared. 'If you do, I will find a way of making you pay. He is under my protection.' Against a vampire, his threat sounded pathetic, but he meant it.

'The friend of Mel Foster is also my friend,' added Eve.

'Blood-hoarders!' Viorica flew off down the stairs in a flurry of red silk skirts. 'I hate you!'

Relieved that the vampire was gone, Mel and Eve entered Dr Foster's bedroom. Cain was gently brushing back the doctor's white hair, tutting as bits of it came away in his fist. Abel was examining the patient's skin where it had flaked.

'We've never seen anything like it,' Abel said in a low voice. 'You found him like this?'

'Yes – but there's more.' Mel quickly explained about the major general.

'He exploded, you say, when you touched him?' Abel crossed his arms, fingers tapping.

'Yes. I'm sure he was nothing more than paint and . . . and whatever was used to make him come alive. Somehow someone had brought him out of the painting in the drawing room.' Mel moved closer. The doctor looked worse than ever. A new tear had appeared on his neck, but it wasn't bleeding, just gaping wide and showing tendons like canvas threads beneath.

'But you saw – or thought you saw – the doctor walking along the street this morning?' asked Cain.

'Yes. But it can't have been him, now I think about it.' Mel recalled the sharply-dressed, quick-moving man he had pursued. 'He looked much younger for a start. I only thought it was him because he looked exactly like the portrait of Dr Foster in the orphanage.' Then the penny dropped. 'Portrait!'

'That's it!' Abel moved to the window. 'That's the link. If you fought a painting of a major general, I can see no logical reason why you cannot also have chased after a portrait patron. Who was the army gentleman?'

'Someone called Anson.'

'Cain? You're the military expert.'

The rough brother scratched his head. 'Last century, I believe. Distant connection of Lady Bracknell's. Long dead.'

'So there was no living body behind that portrait – just paint.' Abel leaned against the window sill, framed by the wafting white net curtains, an angel in his clouds.

'Can the process be reversed?' asked Mel.

The twins exchanged one of their looks.

'We don't know yet, mate,' said Cain gruffly. 'We don't know how it was done. Damned clever person behind this.'

'Or someone with occult powers – this has the taint of forbidden knowledge,' added Abel.

Mel squeezed his hands into fists, feeling powerless. 'So what can we do for Dr Foster?'

'Look after him – and try to capture his double.' Abel drew the heavier damask curtains to aid the patient's sleep. 'Perhaps if we have them both in the same room we will be able to work out how to restore your friend to health.'

'Let him rest now. When he wakes, we'll question him. See what he remembers about the process – and about you.' Cain's eyes shone from under his jutting brows. 'We still have to work out what part *you* play in all this.'

Mel had a horrid thought. 'But if this was done to Dr Foster simply because he had a portrait, does it not mean anyone whose image is captured and sent to the

Chief Butler is vulnerable?' He remembered what Lady Bracknell had said about photographing the orphans. 'Oh, Kingdom Brunel, that's it – that's part of the plan! Lady Bracknell said that now Burlington has rounded up all the powerful creatures who could stand against him, he's moving on to crushing human enemies. He's using pictures and photographs to build his army. Lady Bracknell called Dr Foster one of the first recruits – now I know what she meant!'

'What use is an army if they just explode on touch?' asked Eve.

Mel shrugged. 'The soldier was just a portrait, made for show. I'm not sure what would happen to doubles if there are real people behind them.'

Abel snapped his fingers. 'Do you have an image of yourself somewhere, Master Foster?'

Mel shook his head. 'No. There's only a description on the Wanted posters, no picture.'

'No photograph?'

'No, sir.'

'Cain, who else here has a picture of them out in the world?'

'We've never sat for a portrait.' Cain counted his points off on his fingers. 'All photographs we have taken are here and have never left the house. Mademoiselle Frankenstein has been in the North Pole, so she's probably safe.'

'The mummy?' asked Eve.

'He might have been photographed as part of his excavation and later auction,' admitted Abel, 'but it would be hard to tell him apart from the others in the museum's collection.'

'As for our vampire, there's likely to be a portrait of Lady Dracula, but that'll be in her castle in Transylvania. I think we're safe,' concluded Cain.

'No, we're not,' said Mel. 'Don't you remember? Inky and Nightie were photographed at the bottom of a garden. They said that story appeared in all the journals. Anyone could find their picture in an old edition and use it.'

'Stephenson's Rocket! I'd overlooked them. They must be ordered to stay out of sight.' Abel strode between the bed and the door. 'Burlington moves quickly. If he knows Mel is connected to these creatures, all he has to do is work out how to get at Mel through them.'

'But he already has Dr Foster's image. That's one hostage already,' said Mel.

'Then we need to move even more swiftly than Burlington and his allies,' said Abel.

Mel met Eve's worried eyes. Stepping out of doors now was even more dangerous: one photographic plate taken and their lives were forfeit. London was about to turn into a vast prison – every image captured would keep their originals in slavery to Burlington.

Noticing the grim silence, Abel stopped pacing. 'Do not be downcast, ladies and gentlemen! Under this roof are gathered four of the most extraordinary creatures ever born: a giantess, our shape-shifting vampire, and two of the best brains in the world.'

'And most modest.' Cain winked at Mel.

Abel carried on as if he had not heard. 'The boy was right when he said earlier that we must fight back.'

'We certainly can't wait,' agreed Cain. 'Many innocent lives will be at risk.'

On the move again, Abel clicked his fingers in time to his pacing and Cain cracked his knuckles, circling in the opposite direction. The twins thinking was a percussive experience.

Stopping nose to nose with his brother, Abel said, 'London is about to be besieged by Burlington's monstrous pictures.' He poked his brother in the sternum. 'You fight fire with fire.'

'Monsters with monsters.' Cain punched Abel in the chest, making him fall back.

'Exactly!' panted Abel, rubbing his ribs.

'We might be the last hope of this London of yours,' said Eve. She poked the fire and added another shovel of coal. Sparks flitted up the chimney.

'Perhaps the whole world, mademoiselle,' mused Abel. 'Burlington won't stop at Dover.'

The sense of being hunted was growing. Mel moved to the window and peered out. The guest room looked on to the courtyard and the stables. The monster fairies were paddling in the fountain, while the mummy peeled potatoes by the back door to the kitchen. It was deceptively peaceful. 'We can't sit here doing nothing. Yet if we go out, we risk our images being captured. What can we do about that?' he asked.

'A uniform, to hide our identities,' said Abel, coming to stand at Mel's right shoulder.

'We need to hide our faces at the very least,' added Cain.

'A mask,' suggested Eve from the far side of the room.

'Yes, like highwaymen wear. Excellent idea, mademoiselle.' Abel applauded her.

'We still have those black clothes from that housebreaking job last year,' said Cain. 'And some spare cloth.'

'Housebreaking?' asked Mel.

'You don't want to know.' Cain grinned.

'In the cause of scientific progress, naturally,' added Abel.

'Naturally,' echoed Mel.

Abel rubbed his hands. 'You are right, Cain: they'll be perfect. Master Foster can see to the alterations as his penance for running out of the house this morning.'

'Happy to help. How many do you need?' asked Mel. He had been taught to whip up a flag from scraps of material in a gale-force storm, so altering a few uniforms shouldn't take long.

'Four. My brother and I, Mademoiselle Frankenstein, and Lady Dracula.' Abel turned to leave. 'Come, brother, let us fetch the garments from the attic.'

'Don't forget one for me, sir!' called Mel.

Abel stopped at the threshold, brow arched. 'You? You will not need one, Master Foster.'

'But I want to fight!' Mel could not imagine sitting tucked up in the house while his allies fought the Chief Butler's army.

Abel shook his head, not deigning to argue. 'Too puny.'

Cain shuffled past and clapped Mel on the back. 'Bad luck.'

Eve patted Mel's head, making his teeth rattle. 'You must stay safe.'

He shook her off. 'But Eve, I don't want to stay safe. I want to beat the Chief Butler!'

'*Non*, *non*, you can't.' She looked very upset that he had even suggested it. 'I lost my father – I cannot lose you too.' She quickly followed the brothers out.

'Eve!' Mel glared at the closed door, furious that his friend had sided with the Jekylls. Until now, Eve and he had been in this together: he refused to be sidelined. '*Non*' was not going to be the last word on his destiny.

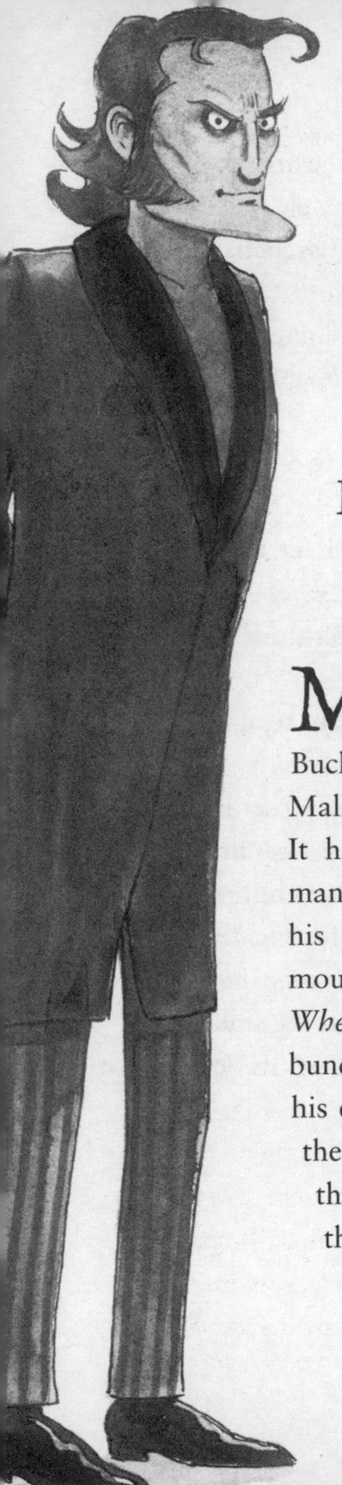

Chapter Twelve

Rain, Steam and Speed

Mr Copperfield stood at one of the windows of the throne room in Buckingham Palace, looking down the Mall. The crowd at the gates was growing. It had started yesterday with a solitary man, well-dressed, gold watch chain across his stomach and a magnificent droopy moustache, who held up a sign reading *Where is the Queen?* He had soon been bundled away by the Monster Patrol, but his example had encouraged others to do the same. They began arriving in twos and threes overnight, and by this morning the crowd had swelled to hundreds. They chanted, 'Down with the Demon Butler!' and their placards all asked variations on the same question: where was the monarch? *Alive, alive-O?* asked one sign, held by a man with a cockle barrow. He was managing to do a good trade while making his protest, something for which Mr Copperfield had to admire him. The crowd had the mood of a determined audience at a boxing match, ready for violence if it came.

'Oh dear, oh dear: this is not going to go down well. His mood is foul enough since he lost the boy again,' muttered Mr Copperfield. The whole palace had heard Burlington rage against Mel Foster's rescuers. New descriptions were being circulated – it was a priority to bring in those who had dared snatch the boy from Burlington's grasp.

The door from the royal apartments banged against the wall, chipping the plaster *fleur-de-lis* on the wall.

'What's that, man?' Burlington swept in, dropped his scarlet dressing gown and got into the Trafalgar fountain. A dapper gentleman followed, holding a linen towel ready for his master. Dressed in the pinstripes and cutaway coat of the mid part of the century, Copperfield guessed the valet was another of the bizarre picture apparitions who had taken up residence in the Palace lately. The 'not-quite-people', he called them. They gave him the creeps. Their expressions were fixed, no matter what terrible thing they were doing. Buttering bread or torturing a prisoner, their faces registered no change. The only time he had ever seen any emotion was when their own existence was threatened by one of Burlington's red rages. Then they ran and screamed like everyone else, trying to get out of his way.

Burlington put his head under one of the water spouts and rubbed his hair vigorously. Then he clicked his fingers. 'Dr Foster. Towel. Now!'

The valet handed him the linen cloth, then offered him a robe.

'In a moment, Foster. I want to hear what Copperfield was saying first. Go on, speak up! I heard you say this wasn't going to go down well.' The Chief Butler shook his head, flinging sparkling droplets of water around the room.

'It is the crowd, sir. I was merely anticipating your displeasure,' said Mr Copperfield humbly.

'And you are right to do so.' Burlington got out of his odd choice of bathing pool like a huge crow fluttering away from a quick dip in a birdbath. He kicked the valet out of his path. 'But they will be gone very soon. I have called out my army.'

Mr Copperfield gulped. 'I see, sir. Have you considered that maybe a personal appearance by Her Majesty on the balcony might effectively disperse them without resorting to force?'

'Yes.'

Mr Copperfield felt a surge of hope. 'So . . . so Her Majesty will emerge and prove she is well?'

'No.' Burlington drew on a long-tailed blue satin coat

and tight fawn breeches. 'I considered – and rejected. It is not for queens to come at the call of commoners.'

'Indeed, sir.' Mr Copperfield cursed himself for his inability to stand up to this terrifying man. Where did the Chief Butler get his power? How had this single person managed to overturn centuries of parliamentary monarchy and hold the whole Empire in his thrall? He'd locked up or recruited monsters so there was no one left with the power to match him; now he was turning on the population.

'I've decided to unveil the next stage in my plan. Thanks to Dorian Gray and Herbert Wallace, I have a splendid army to deal with these grumblers.' Burlington threw open the balcony doors. 'Ah, I hear my troops approaching. Come: you should witness this.'

Reluctantly, Mr Copperfield followed the Chief Butler out on to the balcony. The people at the front, seeing movement at the Palace, increased their cries:

'Show us the Queen!'

'Long live Her Majesty!'

'Down with butlers!'

Burlington smiled, sharp fingernails tapping the stone railing.

At the back of the crowd, though, something else was happening. Mr Copperfield could hear screams and shouts. People were dashing in all directions, heading for the trees of the royal parks. Then he saw what was making them run. It couldn't be! King Charles I was riding down the Mall on a white horse, at the head of a squad of cavaliers, extravagant plumes fluttering in the breeze, sabres twirling. Those who did not move fast enough were trampled, or struck down by swords.

'I do like the cavalry – so full of energy.' Burlington laughed as a child was tossed into a hedge and its mother slashed by a blade. What had been painted soldiers, animated by the butler's allies, were now causing real bloodshed.

'Please, sir!' Mr Copperfield's outrage overcame his prudence. 'This must stop! The people will disperse quietly.' He grabbed the lapel of the Chief Butler's jacket to give him a shake. 'There's no need for anyone to die!'

With a swipe of an arm, Burlington threw him off. Mr Copperfield's old bones crunched as he hit the doorframe. 'Careful, Copperfield, you overstep. Horrified protests I enjoy, but if you lay another finger on me, you will end up in pieces.' His eyes gleamed with malicious joy, his black tongue flickered over his lips. 'Ripped apart so even your dearest friends cannot work out how to fit you in your coffin!'

Sprawled in the corner of the balcony, Mr Copperfield, feeling all his eight decades, held up both hands in entreaty. He was too old to fight such a fellow. The butler was clearly no ordinary man – he had inhuman strength and no mercy. He revelled in suffering, laughing as innocents were slaughtered. He was more of a monster than any he had captured.

The private secretary's brief rebellion crushed, Mr Burlington turned back to the carnage before the gates.

'Wonderful! My troops are even better than I anticipated. I must commend Gray for bringing these possibilities to my attention.' Burlington chuckled as the cockle barrow overturned and the placard was held aloft, pierced on the end of Charles I's sword. 'Ah, and here come the reinforcements! No escape that way, ladies and gentlemen.' Burlington leaned over the rail to watch a flotilla of young women, all dressed in greys and blues, their huge powdered hair and hats in the style of the eighteenth-century artist, Gainsborough, advanced in formation on a little group who had tried to escape towards Green Park. At first glance, the ladies looked harmless beauties – until in a synchronised move they drew long knives from the folds of their skirts. Their serenity as they slashed at those who tried to escape was ghastly. They betrayed no more emotion than an infant stepping on ants. A man hit back at one of them with a stout branch ripped from a tree. His target swayed on her feet but showed no other sign of injury, bonnet ribbons fluttering gaily. He hit her again – and again – but the branch splintered and the man disappeared into a huddle of elegant furies wielding knives.

Mr Copperfield sobbed. He was watching the destruction of British lives and liberty – and there was nothing he could do to prevent it. Burlington truly was a demon.

Then something grey streaked across the sky and dived into the knot of bladed ladies. The man was dragged free, borne off by a huge wolf. The creature made for the cover of the bandstand where a few people had taken refuge from the fighting, leaving him there for others to pull up to the safety of the platform. The wolf disappeared back into the fray.

'Interesting: a vampire,' murmured Burlington, eyes following the wolf. 'There are more monster rebels than I realized.'

Next, a remarkable horseless carriage came speeding down the Mall, heading directly for the worst of the fighting. Long and sleek like a black panther, it roared towards the cavalry, driving a wedge between them and the protesters. Screeching to a halt, three figures leapt out: a giant female, an elegant young man of medium stature and another built like a coal miner, stocky and strong. They were all wore black, tight-fitting uniforms. Face-masks obscured their features.

The tallest did not bother with any weapon but her gloved hands. She began flinging riders from their mounts, scaring the horses into bolting from the field of combat. She went through the soldiers like a scythe through wheat.

The other two wielded firearms. They shot at the Gainsborough ladies but the bullets made little impact on the women, releasing puffs of powder but not slowing them down. The marksmen retreated to take cover by the carriage, their alarm clear. They had been expecting more from their weapons. The ladies reformed their platoon and arrowed towards them, blades aimed at their throats. Mr Copperfield feared the fighters were about to be overwhelmed, but then the horseless carriage growled into action again. The driver – bizarrely, his face was completely bandaged, neck tag fluttering – charged at the ladies, driving through their midst, scattering them left and right like bowling pins. Those who went under the wheels were crushed to a powder, those struck at speed ripped apart, an arm flapping off a body like an old advertisement disintegrating in the wind and rain.

Burlington's expression soured. 'I see Mel Foster's protectors have arrived – I knew they were up to more than just saving him. Time to bring out the heavy weapons.' He gave a sharp whistle that seemed to go on and on. Then Mr Copperfield realized that the butler himself had stopped whistling; the sound was coming now from further off. Pulling himself to his feet, Mr Copperfield searched the horizon. There was a strange mist on Birdcage Walk to his right. It rapidly ate up the lawns of St James's Park, approaching the Palace by the shortest route. A black smokestack appeared, a smear of red on a shadowy engine. Ducks, swans and rabbits darted out of its path. Gouts of steam billowed into the air and rain began to pour down on the fighters, turning the sunny morning to a damp dull cloud of confusion. With gathering dread, Mr Copperfield realized what it was. He had seen it before in the National Gallery.

'Get out of the way!' he shouted, pointing at the approaching menace. 'It's the Great Western Express and it's coming right at you!'

Mel feared he would be too late. The raven had brought word of the trouble outside the Palace and the Jekylls had zoomed off with Eve and Viorica ten minutes ago, taking the mummy to drive them. When they left, Mel donned his uniform, made in secret, and hurried to the nearest Underground station, ignoring the protests of the butler and cheered on by the monster fairies' excited squeals. Each stop on the Metropolitan line seemed an insult as he counted the minutes it took to arrive, and he had neglected to consider that sitting in a railway carriage dressed in a black uniform and mask might not go down well with the British public. The gentleman opposite had raised his newspaper so he did not have to look at him and two ladies whispered, heads together, all the way. When they reached Green Park station, one of them rushed over to the Monster Patrolman on duty, but Mel did not linger to be caught.

Bounding up the stairs and emerging from the station, Mel found he was the only one heading for the Palace as he forced his way through crowds streaming in the opposite direction. Fortunately, his uniform and mask encouraged people to give him a wide berth so he was able to reach the battle right outside the Palace.

He paused to catch his breath, sheltering at the edge of the park. The top of the Mall was a gory confusion of wet paint, ghoulish portrait ladies with limbs half detached, stampeding horses, and unseated cavaliers brandishing silver swords. Charles I was rallying the remainder of his troops against the Monster Resistance. Somewhere to Mel's right he could hear a man shouting a frantic warning. Glimpsing movement on the balcony, Mel saw an elderly chap pointing to the east before being battered aside by a brute of a fellow. It didn't look good, but the old gentleman was too far away for Mel to save. What had he been trying to warn them about? Climbing on a fence post Mel tried to see over the heads of the fighters. A grey storm was sweeping upon them, like a squall at sea, but there was something hidden in the mist. The shape never resolved itself in any clearer detail, never detached from the smoky haze, but it was travelling fast with a shrill whistle and the regular strokes of a high-speed train. Mel could sense its heaviness, its power.

He saw Eve and the twins, clearing people out of its path.

Why don't you just touch it? The moment he had come into contact with the major general, the soldier had exploded. He couldn't understand why they hadn't got rid of the threat.

The twins must have been thinking the same thing.

'Maybe it has to be skin to skin!' shouted Abel to Cain, gesturing to the others to fan out in case the locomotive changed direction. Taking the middle position, Abel took off his glove.

With a scream, the black stack of the train bore down on Abel, rain coming ahead as a foretaste of its attack. Abel reached out, made contact – and was catapulted ten feet in the air, spinning, spinning . . . He fell against the black iron railings of the Palace with a sickening impact, head at an odd angle.

'Abel!' bellowed Cain.

The train carried on unaffected, driving the crowd towards the cavalry's swords.

Why hadn't Abel's touch worked? Why was the train not returned to paint? Mel had no time to calculate the risks: he just had to stop it. The train was about to cause a massacre. He dashed forward into its path, before it could run down a family whom Eve was trying to shelter. Dwarfed by the cloud, Mel punched the Express right in the centre of the circular front of its locomotive.

His fist met . . . nothing. Simultaneously, with a huge hurricane blast, the train erupted, throwing Mel flailing backwards against the horse that bore Charles I. The white stallion detonated, the shockwave taking the Stuart king with it. Mel ended up on the pavement, covered in a sticky layer of wet oil streaked with white, grey and red.

'What the blazes just happened?' Mel muttered dazedly, head spinning.

Before he got his answer, he was scooped off the ground by Eve and shoved in the back of the horseless carriage – a wonderful vehicle he barely had time to register. Cain was already inside, Abel on his lap. Eve jumped in the seat beside the driver, her legs curled up to fit.

'*Allez*! *Allez*!' she ordered the mummy.

The Egyptian put his foot down on the pedal and the vehicle screeched away from the battlefield. Mel glanced out of the rear window. The explosion had cleared a path for people to escape. The protesters were running for Piccadilly, a wolf leading them to safety, clearing Monster Patrolmen out of their path. A few of the more damaged Gainsborough ladies, no longer in a fit shape to take orders, limped after them, dragging torn limbs behind them like macabre bunting. Mel wished he could put the pictures out of their misery but the mummy had no intention of stopping for Mel to return them to paint. He drove up Haymarket and Shaftesbury Avenue with reckless flair, demonstrating that four thousand years of being dead had not dented his reflexes. With much application of the horn and rude gesticulating at cabbies who didn't move out of the way fast enough, he got them back to Bloomsbury in record time.

'Quick, get us under cover!' urged Cain.

Mr Marley must have been watching, for the gates of the mews round the back opened and the carriage drove straight into the stable. The wooden loosebox slid back into place, complete with a fake horse-head leaning over the top to graze on a bag of oats.

'Mademoiselle Frankenstein, take Abel!' bellowed Cain.

'Where?' Eve asked, taking the unconscious brother from Cain's arms.

'To the laboratory. Put him on the table.'

'But Monsieur Cain, he is dead, no?'

Mel hurried in behind Eve, turning on the lights.

'It's not too late – it can't be too late.' Cain swiped all the equipment off the dissection table to make room. 'I have to force a change.' He grabbed the collecting flask from under the still, tugged off the mask and dribbled some of the blue liquid between his brother's lips before taking a swig himself.

'But if you change bodies,' Mel protested, 'might you not die instead?'

Cain's features were already blurring. He smiled grimly at Mel. 'I might.'

The body on the table started shaking and jerking. Cain let out an inhuman shriek of pain, his neck twisting and writhing. He dropped the bottle. It smashed on the ground, hissing as the liquid burned through the tiles.

'Nooo!' shouted Abel, his throat distending, veins

standing out as his bones cracked and popped into their new shapc. He shook like he was being electrocuted. Cain threw his arms wide, skin seething. 'Brother, don't!' screamed Abel.

Eve caught Cain as he fell forward, his glossy auburn hair flopping over his now delicate features.

Abel sat up with a gasp. 'Aaargh!' He seized his own neck, checking his spine. 'What have you done?' He leapt off the table and plucked Cain from Eve's arms. 'How dare you risk yourself for me!' He howled in anguish, rocking the body to and fro.

Cain's eyes fluttered open. 'Careful,' he whispered, 'you might break something. Again.'

With a sob of relief, Abel laid him on the sofa. 'Don't you ever risk your life for mine, you hear?'

Cain smiled. 'Do not tell me you would not do the same thing for me.'

Abel snorted. 'I'm not as nice as you, remember?'

Cain gave a weak chuckle, then put his hands to his ribs. 'Ouch! I feel the impact of every railing. Even with the exchange I think I've got a few bruises.'

Abel collapsed into an old armchair. His coarse hair stood up in sweaty spikes. 'Tell me what happened after.'

'After you came out worse in a confrontation with the 11.15 to Paddington?' Cain waved at Mel who was sweeping up the shards of glass with a broomstick. 'The boy here had the magic touch – destroyed the train with a nicely-judged punch.'

'He succeeded where we could not. That must be his gift – the reason why Burlington is so keen to round him up.'

'Exactly. Something about Mel Foster defeats those paint monsters. We made an almost fatal error thinking it could be done by any one of us.'

Mel found two pairs of green eyes fixed on him. Now he had spent longer with the twins he had come to notice one difference between them: whichever body they were in, Cain's eyes were a little paler, softer in expression, than his brother's. Cain was also the one with the sense of humour; Abel was more waspish. Mel was glad he had a method of telling them apart now. The shape exchange was monstrously confusing.

'It seems that way,' Mel admitted. 'I also did for Charles I and his horse.'

'Everyone else who touched them was hurt,' said Eve, taking Mel's hands and checking for injuries, 'bleeding from real wounds; only Mel was able to destroy them.'

'So we have some answers,' mused Cain, 'but they only lead to more questions.'

'I have one question,' said Eve, glaring at Mel. 'Why were you there at all, Mel Foster? You were supposed to be here – safe!'

'Not that we aren't grateful to you for saving the day,' added Cain with a wry smile, rubbing his ribs.

'I'm not very good at following orders.' Mel could

see that Eve was genuinely upset that he had put himself in the path of danger. 'Sorry, Eve.'

She surprised him with a tight hug, which was an unintended punishment as she still didn't know her own strength. 'You saved me from that train, but first I died a thousand times seeing you stand before that terrible engine. You are impossible. We tell you, "Be safe", but you will not stay out of danger. These paint creatures do not harm you but there are many other things that can. You must stay close to me in future, agreed?'

'I'll try, but I can't promise.'

Eve gave an exasperated huff, but before she could muster another argument, a weary wolf slunk into the laboratory. It circled twice on the hearthrug before lying down and tugging a blanket over itself with its teeth. Its skin shimmered and resolved into the curled-up form of Viorica.

'You could have at least given me a lift home,' she grumbled.

'You did well. Thank you,' said Abel gruffly.

'It was . . . interesting.' She yawned. 'I'm pleased to see you alive. When I wake up, I'll tell you what I saw on the way back. You are not going to like it.' With that, she fell into a motionless sleep, chest not moving.

Abel cracked his knuckles and stretched. 'I like a good punch-up, gets the circulation flowing, but that battle was messy. Too many civilians caught up in it.'

'We are going to need new tactics,' offered Cain

wearily. 'We must work out how far the boy's power goes. Touching Dr Foster wakes him, but does not cure him.'

'If only the Foster double had been in the battle, we could've captured it,' said Abel. 'Then seen what happens when Master Foster touched it.'

'He might kill the original,' suggested Cain. 'He explodes them, remember?'

'Don't remind me,' muttered Mel.

'But it might snap the link and cure the doctor,' persisted Abel.

'True.' Cain closed his eyes. 'I think . . . I'd best . . . sleep on it.'

Leaving the vampire and Cain to recuperate, Mel, Eve and Abel crept from the room, closing the door softly behind them.

Chapter Thirteen
Doppelgänger

Abel loped off to his library to research the mystery, leaving Mel and Eve alone in the corridor.

Eve folded her arms and just looked at Mel, making him squirm.

He scuffed his toe on the carpet. 'I'm sorry, Eve, if I worried you.'

'You always worry me, Mel.' Her mismatched eyes were full of misery. 'I leave you safe and, *voilà*, there you are in the centre of trouble. But you are so little – so breakable.'

'I'm just human.'

'But you are *my* human. My family.'

He felt a swirl of warmth at her words. He had never had anyone so completely on his side, not even Dr Foster. 'And you're mine. We'll look after each other.'

She nodded and brushed a tear off her cheek.

He reached for her hand, feeling the scars under his fingers. 'And as it seems I'm the only one who can fight those painting creatures, perhaps we should go and ask Dr Foster if he can explain why I have this power?'

The doctor had spent the day sleeping peacefully. Mr Marley was keeping vigil, floating by the bed with a doleful expression that would persuade even someone recovering that they were heading for the graveyard.

'How is he?' asked Mel, knowing now what to expect from the ghost. Eve followed him in, making surprising little noise for so large a person.

'Oh, sir, he is almost in my world. His spirit hovers on the edge of death – that undiscovered country from whose bourn no traveller returns.' Marley frowned. 'Except me and the other ghosts.'

'I'd like to talk to him a moment.'

Marley smiled sadly. 'Be my guest.'

'Just Eve and me.'

With a sniff, the ghost drifted off through the wall, his chains following him like a long tail.

Mel took a seat on the bed. The doctor barely seemed to be breathing. His slightly hooked nose rose out of his narrow grey cheeks, too sharp. Dr Foster had always had a flush of good humour and energy about him. That all seemed drained. With a glance at Eve, Mel gingerly reached out for the doctor's hand. He brushed a knuckle with his fingertip.

Dr Foster gasped and his eyes fluttered open. They

swivelled briefly at the ceiling then turned to find Mel. A smile crinkled the corners of his mouth under the white fringe of moustache and beard.

'Melchizedek. My boy.' His eyes turned to Eve in consternation. 'Good gracious!'

'This is Eve Frankenstein. She saved you, don't you remember?'

'The large lady at the gate?'

'That's her.'

The doctor swallowed and remembered his manners. 'Delighted to make your acquaintance, miss.'

'How are you, monsieur?' asked Eve, sitting down on a sturdy chair to make her height less imposing.

Dr Foster sighed. 'Not feeling all here, to be honest.'

'Do you remember any more about what happened to you – how you came to be like this?'

'What has happened to me?' Dr Foster lifted one worn hand, studying it with grim fascination.

'We think that the Chief Butler has found a way of linking your life to a double taken from your portrait,' explained Mel.

'A doppelgänger!' exclaimed Dr Foster, letting his arm fall back on the cover. 'I've read about such things, but do you mean someone has actually managed to do this?'

'I'm afraid so, sir, but we don't know how. We thought you might be able to give us some clues.'

Dr Foster closed his eyes, his energy fading, chest

barely rising with each intake of breath. Pressing his fingertips to the doctor's pulse, Mel willed a little more of his own strength into the patient. It appeared to work, for the doctor's breathing eased and his lids lifted. 'I remember now. Lady Bracknell summoned me to her house at one in the morning – told me she had information about you. My picture from the orphanage was propped against a wall in her drawing room. The last thing I remember was looking at it when I felt a tug in my chest, strong, painful, like I was being turned inside out. I blacked out. The next thing I clearly remember is you waking me up.'

'You're a medical man, sir. Can you think of any explanation?'

Dr Foster plucked at the cover fretfully. 'One hears rumours at the Royal Society, but I usually dismiss them as the worst sort of sensational tales.'

'What sort of rumours?'

'Dark knowledge coming out of the furthest corners of the Empire – things that should remain shut away in the tombs of the ancients. First we found long-hidden monsters, then we found the knowledge to create more by our own devices. There have been whispers of scientists uncovering these secrets and using them to cross the boundaries of nature, releasing powers they don't understand.'

Dr Foster's words conjured up for Mel a vision of a flickering torch lighting up the dusty tomb of an ancient king, curses falling on those who looted the grave goods; parchments filled with obscure writings painstakingly decoded by scholars; old secrets put to the test in modern laboratories.

'Have you met anyone who has done this?' Eve asked in a hushed tone.

'There was this patient of mine – a Mr Dorian Gray,' continued Dr Foster. 'He suffered from a debilitating medical condition for which there was no cure. Then one day, he suddenly stopped coming to my surgery. Fearing the worst, I called on him to see how he was doing. He welcomed me in, visibly much improved – I'd venture even to say that he was in perfect health, which should have been impossible. While we talked of this and that over a glass of wine, I noticed a gap on the library wall where his portrait usually hung. I asked if he had been burgled. He laughed and said no, he had swapped his life for the portrait's. Made no sense to me at the time – he always was a rum fellow – but now I wonder.'

Mel let the doctor rest for a moment. 'If you can transfer bad health from human to painting, logically it might also work in reverse,' he whispered to Eve.

'Burlington's army is invulnerable, then?' asked Eve. 'Harm a soldier and the original suffers?'

'That would explain the doctor's link to his portrait. When Burlington hits the double, Dr Foster must take the injury. But can I free the doctor by touching his double? I just don't know.'

'Monsieur,' Eve asked the doctor after a few minutes had passed containing nothing more than the rattle of carriages outside and the warmth of the sun coming through the half-drawn curtains, 'can you tell us why Mel Foster has this power over the paintings? The Chief Butler must have suspected something, as he was already hunting him before we discovered it. What does he know that we do not?'

'I'm not sure I can help, but I can tell you what I know about Melchizedek's origins.' The doctor reached for Mel's fingers. 'I would have told you before, but you were too young – and then you were gone to sea.'

'Tell me now, sir,' said Mel.

'Your mother was a sweet girl of good family. She told me that she had run away because she was afraid of her husband.' Dr Foster's voice dropped. 'Actually, that's not quite what she said. "I'm afraid of what he has become," she told me. She called him the Inventor.'

'The Inventor?'

'Just that – no name, no description. I assumed he must reside in one of the universities – Oxford, most likely, as I found her on the westward road from that city heading for Gloucester.'

Mel tried to imagine his mother. 'What did she look like?'

'Long, fair hair, hazel eyes, gentle in spirit.' The doctor's gaze rested on Mel's face. 'I would guess you take more after your father in looks, but your spirit reminds me of hers. I grieved when she passed, as I had become very fond of her in the short time of our acquaintance – such a lovely smile when she held you. Her main concern was that I should check that you had not been injured. There was some mishap at your birth that left you with that brand on your chest. Poor girl was quite distraught about it – talked a jumble about storms and experiments, none of it making a jot of sense.'

Mel rubbed the shiny red patch of the key-shaped burn below his collar.

'She said the key attracted bad luck and begged me to get rid of it. Of course, I did no such thing – it was the only possession you had once she died.'

'Where is it now?' asked Eve.

'In my desk at home.'

But it wasn't. The monster fairies had already searched and found nothing more than a bag of sweets. Burlington's people had got there first.

Dr Foster was still thinking of Mel's mother. 'Alas, she died before I could help her reconcile with her family. I made enquiries, of course.'

'Enquiries?'

'For a gentleman of science who had recently mislaid an expectant wife. I was anticipating your stay at the orphanage to be very short, as his wife going missing is hardly something even the most distracted scholar could fail to notice.' The doctor's expression turned inward, caught up in the past. 'But none of my acquaintance admitted to hearing of someone styling himself the Inventor.' His gaze sharpened. 'All I had to go on was a key and a child.'

Mel turned that idea over in his mind. The key had to mean something if his mother had bothered to tie it around his neck, but why did she then ask for it to be thrown away? 'She never explained the key?'

'No, she never mentioned it again after I promised to get rid of it.'

'Do you have a picture of her, sir?'

'I'm afraid I don't.'

'Maybe that's just as well.' Mel did not want to think of the horror of confronting his portrait mother in battle.

'Is there anything you need?' asked Eve.

'Just a cure for what ails me.' Dr Foster gave a weary sigh. 'Dashed awkward being unable to do anything to help.'

Eve smoothed his pillow. 'We hope the twins will cure you. The Jekylls have brilliant minds.'

Dr Foster closed his eyes for a final time. 'I knew their father. I asked him once if he could be this Inventor fellow, but he denied it in strongest terms. Odd chap, Mr Jekyll senior: he had this most unpleasant servant man called Hyde about the place. Never knew he had twins, thought he only had the one boy, but then he always was a secretive gentleman.'

At dinner that evening, the Monster Resistance members gathered in the dining room to discuss the army of invulnerable doubles. The Jekylls had taken the precaution of removing all family portraits; only patches of darker wallpaper outlined where they had been.

'You never know,' said Cain from his sofa as he watched his brother heave the last picture out.

'How are you feeling, sir?' asked Mel.

'Still a little tender about the ribs, but when we exchange tomorrow I believe even that will be gone. Abel should not be troubled.'

Mel perched by Cain's velvet-slippered feet. He felt able to ask Cain questions that he would not risk with the quick-tempered Abel. 'So, do you change every day?'

'Most days. More often when there is need either to go out in genteel society – that's this form – or use our strength – that's the other. But swapping is a painful process, as you will remember from your healing draft.'

Mel clutched his stomach. 'Do you mean . . . am I going to change too?'

Cain laughed. 'No, Master Foster. You would have to drink the medicine regularly to trigger changes, and that would not be with another person, but with the other side of you that lies hidden in the dark places of your soul. You might not retain your good sense and moral courage if you let that out. That is what happened to our father – he divided into two personalities and called the other Hyde. Hyde defeated him in the end.'

'What about you two?'

'Fortunately, Abel and I were born with an ability to swap between ourselves. I can't claim either of us are saintly people, but somewhere in the exchange the good and bad seem to balance each other out. It is certainly an improvement on what our father experienced.'

That reminded Mel of the conversation he and Eve had had with Dr Foster, so he told Cain what he had learned about his parents.

'Interesting.' Cain brushed his fringe off his forehead, resting back on the plump pillow. 'A man called the Inventor. I seem to have heard something about him before, but I can't put my finger on it. I must ask Abel. It could be one of his subjects.'

'You share out memory duties?'

'Of course. More efficient when there is so much to think about. Sometimes I wish we could lodge a library in the air and pull down the knowledge when needed, but until someone invents a way of doing that, we have to make do.'

At that moment, the mummy came in bearing a tray laden with food, lurching a little as he tripped on a trailing bandage. Eve followed with a second platter. The raven flapped in and tapped the gong on the sideboard with its beak, signalling that dinner was served. Before the noise had died away, Viorica materialized in the shadows. Abel returned from his task of picture removal and helped his brother to a seat at the head of the table, taking the place at the foot. Viorica glided to a chair at Cain's right and the mummy put a silver chalice in front of her.

The raven flew down to sit on the elaborate silver fruit bowl in the centre of the table. Shaped like two mermaids holding up a seashell with their tails, a sprinkle of seeds, bread and a few beetles had been put in it for the bird's supper. The insects were still moving about but a sharp black beak pecked up any that tried to escape on to the snowy expanse of linen cloth.

'Ladies and gentlemen,' said Cain. 'To the defeat of the Chief Butler!' He raised his glass of wine to wet his lips. 'Now, I believe it is time we heard the news brought home by the lady here.'

Viorica wiped her mouth delicately on a white napkin, leaving a red smear behind. 'It was not pleasant, returning through London. These Londoners, ignorant peasants, are not kind to animals.'

Mel smiled down at his plate. Personally, he felt they should be allowed to be a little startled to see a vampire wolf in daylight.

'But that is not what I have to tell you. As I crossed the great square – I believe it is called Trafalgar, yes? – I saw the Monster Patrol gathering those who had tried to escape the Mall. They were photographing them; not individual portraits but masses, hundreds, at a time.'

'I see.' Cain twisted the cut-glass vessel in his hand, letting it catch the light on its different facets. 'Burlington is eliminating any chance of opposition. He got to the monsters first and now he is after the ordinary people. If everyone is photographed and labelled, then no one is safe. Step out of line and you get a double taking over your life.'

'He is not leading this part of the operation himself.' Viorica sipped her drink, wrinkling her nose at the day-old blood. 'Instead there was one of his ministers, the man in charge of the Queen's art collection: Dorian Gray.'

'That's the man Dr Foster knew!' exclaimed Mel. 'He cured himself by giving his illness to a portrait.'

'How curious.' Viorica fixed Mel with her unnerving blue gaze. 'He is aided by a scientist called Herbert Wallace. I believe the scientist was the one taking the photographic plates.'

'We know him too. He was there when I found Eve,' said Mel.

'He is an idiot,' observed Eve succinctly.

'At last, some of our information is coming together. Are you sure you weren't caught in the frame as you crossed the square, Lady Dracula?' asked Abel gruffly.

Viorica smiled and slicked her hair behind her ears. 'Very sure.'

'You seem overly confident, madam,' said Cain.

'I am. Vampires do not have reflections. It is

impossible therefore to take our photograph.' She licked her lips, eyes drifting back to Mel. 'One of the benefits of my condition, if anyone would like to join me in it.'

Eve snapped her silver fork. 'Do not even think about converting Mel Foster,' she said. 'He must stay as he is.'

'Indeed,' agreed Abel. 'We need his power; becoming a vampire might kill that.'

Mel felt it was high time he spoke up for himself. 'Actually, sir, my lady, I wasn't even considering it as a career.'

Viorica rubbed the tip of her index finger along the line of her jaw, dipping to the place on her neck where she herself had been first bitten. 'Well, it is something to think about. Being a vampire might be the only safe way to be very soon.'

Mel turned his attention to the chicken pie in front of him and began eating with great concentration.

Cain seemed amused by the exchange. 'So, if I may summarize, ladies and gentlemen?' Abel nodded and shovelled in a forkful of food, chewing with his mouth open. 'The Chief Butler has found a means of trapping the life of people in their images. We do not know if that process is reversible, or whether destroying the double would kill the original. Until we have settled that question, Master Foster's gift cannot safely be used on doubles. However, we do have in the boy a formidable defence against the pure paint creatures – figures from paintings of the past, or of fantasy. He must be in the front line against them.'

Eve held up a hand.

Cain graciously gave way. 'Yes, mademoiselle?'

'But we have seen that force also worked against the creatures to some degree – my fists, the horseless carriage.'

'True. Where it is not safe for Master Foster, we can use more traditional means, but the shortcoming of those is that they tend to disable rather than defeat. We all, I think, remember the Gainsborough ladies.'

A shudder ran round the table. Mel wondered if those damaged paintings were still flapping confusedly around the park.

'Burlington saw what our talented boy here can do: he will be more determined than ever to capture him,' said Cain.

'Wonderful,' muttered Mel.

'He has a hostage in Dr Foster's double, but so far he has not yet used him to draw us out into the open. Abel and I imagine that will be his next move.'

'He might threaten to kill Foster's double just to show us he can,' said Abel. 'That's what I would do if I were him. Keep killing hostages until he forces the boy out of hiding.'

Mel put his knife and fork together on the plate, appetite vanished. 'Can we warn people? If they knew, they could move and blur their image when photographed. Maybe that would stop the connection being made?'

'A good thought,' said Cain. 'We could certainly try to tell them, but I doubt we can be more persuasive than a group of Burlington's thugs threatening to thump them if they spoil the image. However, we must do something.' He turned to the bird. 'Raven, if I print a warning, will you drop them around London, to the newspapers and so on? Maybe someone will be brave enough to publish it.'

The raven squawked its agreement.

'I hate going up against a technology I don't understand. What we really need is an answer as to how this all works,' said Abel.

'Then we must catch one of those doing the photography – this Gray or the idiot Wallace – and make them tell us,' suggested Eve.

'But if they're terrified of Burlington, it will take a lot of pain to make them bleat,' mused Abel.

Eve's eyes widened in alarm. 'We must not descend to torture, Monsieur Abel. We must reason with them, appeal to their better nature.'

'They are in league with Burlington; I think it is safe to say they do not have a better nature,' observed Viorica dryly.

The mummy, who had been waiting quietly by the sideboard to serve dessert, started waving his hands in the air, a bandage unravelling in his excitement.

'Ah: I think our ancient friend here has an idea,' said Cain.

'Do you understand him?' Mel whispered to Eve.

In answer, Eve got up and fetched pencil and paper from the little writing desk in the library. She returned and handed it to the Egyptian. 'This is how we talk in the kitchen.'

The mummy grabbed the pencil and began sketching out chicken scratch pictograms.

'Hieroglyphs,' Cain explained, seeing Mel's puzzled look.

Eyes, crocodiles and cats were now marching across the white page. 'You can read this?'

'Of course. It is a very logical language.'

The mummy finished and passed the paper to Cain.

'Yes, that might work.' Cain made a paper dart and threw it to Abel to read.

'What is his idea?' asked Viorica, looking doubtful that the cook could come up with anything suitable.

'He reminds us that we know someone we can ask – someone who dabbles in occult practices – an expert on the secrets taken from old manuscripts,' explained Cain.

'Who?' asked Mel.

Abel tore his bread roll in two and shoved a big chunk in his mouth. 'The man who dug him up.'

Chapter Fourteen

Egyptian Secrets

According to the mummy, Professor Bellingham was usually to be found in his office in the British Museum. As he was outside their secret circle, the Jekylls decided that he was best approached in the manner of a normal social call, at least until they knew if he was sympathetic to the Resistance. However, Burlington's spies were going to be everywhere. They had to go disguised as an ordinary family on an outing: Cain was to act as an elder brother showing his sister and younger brother around the Egyptian gallery. Viorica and Mel were to play these parts, Mel's identity disguised by a fair wig, a mass of drawn-on freckles and a pair of spectacles.

Mel put the finishing touches to his outfit in front of an audience of Inky and Nightie.

'How do I look?'

'You look very smart,' said Nightie glumly, scratching his belly through his pink gauze dress. Both fairies generally liked anything to do with dressing up, but today they were sitting on the bed like disconsolate castaways on a counterpane island.

'Not like your usual self,' agreed Inky sadly. 'You look posh.'

'Then what's the matter with you two?'

'You get to go out as one of them. We have to stay here to footle.'

'Footle?'

'Do footmen duties.' Inky picked his toenails. 'Even the mummy is allowed to drive.'

Mel searched for something comforting to say. 'Mr Marley stays here.'

'He's a ghost, so he has to – but we don't. We could help.' Inky's big dark eyes filled with hope.

'Ah.' Mel had secretly been very pleased that he had crossed over from third footman to fifth member of the Resistance. The battle outside the Palace had revolutionized his status in the household. As Cain had said at dinner, they needed him on the front line. He could imagine the fairies felt jealous, seeing him promoted ahead of them.

'We want to fight too,' said Nightie.

Mel slid the spectacles on to his nose, finding his transformation from scruffy urchin to earnest schoolboy fascinating. 'But the journals have the photograph of you at the bottom of that girl's garden. If Burlington sees you with us, he might use that against us.' As he spoke, he had the sinking feeling that he sounded like Eve had when she was trying to keep him safe. He vividly recalled how frustrated he had been. Just because the monster fairies were small didn't mean they couldn't be useful. They had already searched Dr Foster's house; it was natural they would want to see more action. 'I tell you what: I'll put in a word for you with the twins – see if there's something you can do.'

The two fairies perked up. 'You're a top chap,' said Nightie, tweaking the silver bow on his beard straight.

'A swell cove,' agreed Inky, doing a backwards somersault off the bed. 'Hadn't you better be going?'

Leaving the two fairies more cheerful than he found them, Mel joined Viorica and elegant Cain inside the horse-drawn carriage parked in front of the house. Rough Abel was already on the driving seat, collar turned up and hat pulled low over his face. He clicked the horse into a steady trot. Mel knew that Eve was standing at the library window, watching them leave. She was furious that she had had to remain behind, but her stature was too distinct to risk bringing her along.

It was only a short journey to the museum, easily walked, but the twins had decided it was best to keep off the streets. There were informers everywhere; no one lingered on the pavements. Instead they hurried between tasks with the urgency of a city under armed siege, praying they would get home before the Monster Patrol scooped them up for photographing.

The carriage jolted around a corner.

'You will both do as I say,' said Cain, glancing out of the rear window to check no one was following.

Viorica snorted and Mel tried to look obedient.

Cain rolled his eyes. 'We'll go in and I'll ask if we can see the Queen of Sheba's mummified cat. Bellingham is working on that at the moment, and the mummy says he likes displaying his finds to interested parties as he always hopes to attract more funds for another expedition.' Cain threaded a diamond tiepin through his green silk cravat to make sure he looked every inch the rich young man.

'I was just wondering,' said Mel curiously, 'does Professor Bellingham know that our mummy is alive?'

A shifty expression passed over Cain's face. He pulled on a pair of black kid gloves. 'Yes . . . and no.'

'What do you mean?' Viorica sounded amused. She looked deceptively sweet today in a violet bonnet and lacy white dress. 'Have you twins been doing something you should not again?'

'Certainly not.' Cain grinned. 'We had nothing to do with our cook's unusual condition. The professor himself animated our mummy without realizing he had done so.'

'Absurd!' scoffed Viorica. 'How could he not know?'

'Simple: there were two mummies taken from the

tomb he excavated. The professor found a recipe in the ancient parchments buried with them which taught him how to restore life to those who had undergone the mummification process. It worked all too well. The first one – our mummy's uncle – took to its renewed life with rather too keen an appetite. The professor had to destroy it when it started doing away with people it didn't like. Being a more peaceable chap, our mummy decided to bide his time until his evil uncle was out of the way. His uncle had killed him once before, in his old life, and he did not want to let him have a second go in his new one. It was during this interval, when he was pretending to be inanimate, that we bought him at auction.'

'That must have been a shock,' laughed Mel, imagining the twins' faces when their mummy got up out of its casket.

'A delightful surprise. The mummy told us what had gone on in the professor's chambers so we decided not to tell Bellingham that his second subject had woken up and was living quite happily as our cook. We agreed that he would in all likelihood take fright and try to destroy our mummy too.'

Mel pieced their reasoning together. 'And because this professor found that secret in the parchments, the mummy thinks he might know of other men, like this Gray person, who have discovered something similar?'

'Yes, and he would have a good idea how Gray would

pull off the transference with a painting double. That is exactly the kind of knowledge the Egyptians would have learned as they delved deep into the chemistry of the soul.'

At the entrance to the museum, Cain jumped out of the carriage to offer his hand to Viorica as she stepped to the ground. Mel leapt lightly down behind her. Abel parked the vehicle under a tree to wait.

The forecourt of the museum was bathed in sunshine; families picnicked in the shade or listened to lectures from tour guides. Two boys in short trousers and white shirts and two girls in blue sailor suits played leapfrog. Mel was just enjoying the sight and wondering if there would be time for him to join in when a pair of Monster Patrolmen turned into the street and came to a stop at the gates, red uniform conspicuous through the black bars. As quickly as if a rainstorm had arrived, the families packed up, the children ran back to their parents and the tour guides ushered their parties into the safety of the museum.

'Come along, sister, brother: I must show you the latest Egyptian finds,' Cain announced hastily, tucking Viorica's hand into the crook of his arm.

Escaping the vigilance of the Patrolmen, they entered the cool, columned foyer.

'Egyptian gallery to the left,' said Cain, marching onwards.

Mel had never been inside the British Museum.

Although it was theoretically for all people, poor orphan boys like him were turned out if they dared enter, so he was fascinated by his first glimpse at its treasures. It looked to him as though many palaces and temples had been dismantled and their plans muddled, so they were now only semi-erected in the high ceilinged rooms, like a puzzle that someone had abandoned as too difficult. A stone basin here, a crocodile headed statue over there, a cracked frieze of dark-haired people standing sideways on one wall, a slab carved with hieroglyphs on another.

'I bet if we put the mummy to arranging this place he'd do a better job,' Mel whispered to Cain.

'I expect he would,' said Cain, smiling at the thought. 'Let us find the professor.' Seeing a gallery warden strolling nearby, Cain approached him. 'Excuse me, can you tell me where I can find the Queen of Sheba's cat?'

The elderly warden consulted his room guide. 'Ah, I'm afraid that it is not on show today, sir. Professor Bellingham is taking some measurements.'

'What a pity. We have come such a long way and I promised my brother and sister that they could see it. Would you be so kind as to take a message to the professor?' Cain passed the man a sizeable tip. 'Tell him that a Master Jekyll is here. He knew my father.'

The warden touched his cap. 'Right away, Master Jekyll. If you and the young lady and gentleman would like to remain here, I'll go and ask if he is available.'

They did not have to wait long. Professor Bellingham

himself returned with the guard. A short, thin man with tanned skin and wisps of prematurely white hair on either side of a bald crown, he approached with hand outstretched. He reminded Mel of a dowager's lapdog he had once seen – it had only had tufts of hair around its ears, and pink vulnerable skin.

'Ah, Master Jekyll, how lovely to meet you again. We met last at the auction, did we not?'

Cain shook hands. 'Yes, sir.'

'I can't tell you how much I have appreciated the support you have shown my work, picking up where your father left off. Without private collectors like you, I could not afford to undertake excavations. I trust the mummy is giving you satisfaction?'

'He is a most valued addition to our collection,' said Cain.

'Quite, quite. Is he keeping well? No rot or disintegration?'

'He's in good shape.'

'I must call on you one day and see how he is doing for myself.' Bellingham now turned to Viorica. 'Forgive my appalling manners, dear lady. I get a little carried away by my interests.'

'My sister, Victoria, and my youngest brother, Derek.'

Derek? Mel supposed he could forgive Cain that as Melchizedek was a very unusual name.

'Charmed.' The old man bowed low over Viorica's

hand, missing the hungry look in her eyes as she contemplated his head so near her fangs. She gave him a tight-lipped smile.

'And young Derek. I had no idea your father had such a large family?'

'Indeed, he kept many things quiet,' Cain said easily.

'Please, sir, would it be possible to see the cat?' asked Viorica, returning them to business.

'Of course, my dear. I know ladies are partial to kittens and pretty things and the boy will enjoy the science behind the mummification process.' Bellingham waggled his white brows at Mel. 'Brains drawn out through the nose and the like.'

Bellingham had them wrong: Viorica was the one who would enjoy such bloody stuff while Mel preferred not to think about it. 'Indeed, sir,' Mel said politely.

Bellingham led them through a door marked *Museum Staff Only* and into the labyrinth of rooms behind the public galleries. His office was in the basement, lit only by high windows which were at pavement level. The room was a glorious mess. Books teetered on shelves, papers slumped in drifts, odd artefacts lay in no apparent order on every available surface. The only clear space was the professor's workbench. On that lay a tightly-bound mummified cat, bold features painted in black on the bandages so that it appeared to be gazing up at the ceiling eerily.

'Oh, how perfect!' exclaimed Viorica.

'Yes, indeed, it is a splendid example, which is why it has been given that rather fanciful name. I doubt it belonged to the Queen of Sheba – it came out of the same tomb as the mummy you now own.'

Cain was examining the manuscript lying beside the cat. He frowned, green eyes glinting with intelligence. Bellingham caught the direction of his gaze and snatched up the parchment, holding it to his chest.

'Forgive the mess. I wasn't expecting visitors.'

Cain folded his arms. 'Professor, was that not a recipe for reanimation?'

The professor paled. 'You . . . you read hieroglyphics?'

'Yes. I have been taught by an expert.'

'Oh dear. You really should not have seen that.' Bellingham looked lost for a moment, then assumed a hectoring tone. 'Let me warn you, young man, of the dangers of transgressing God's holy laws. Life is His gift, not ours. Do not fall into temptation.'

'As you have?' Cain had found his strategy. The professor was up to his old tricks and would do anything to hide the fact, perhaps even give them the answers they needed.

'How can you say that?' blustered Bellingham. 'I was only investigating so I could warn others of the dangers.'

'I thought you had already experienced the dangers once – or so rumour has it.'

Mel had a funny feeling about the Queen of Sheba's

cat. He looked hard at it. Had it just twitched?

'Well, well . . .' Bellingham was floundering.

'So you recognize that there are some secrets that are too dangerous to be widely known – such as, say, reanimating mummies, casting curses, or creating doppelgängers?' asked Cain.

'Naturally, I would never, ever do such a thing. I mean, one would have to be reckless in the extreme to risk waking the dead!'

As Bellingham protested his utter innocence, Mel reached out and touched the cat. He felt a flick of power pass down his arm. The cat's mouth sprang open in a silent miaow, head twisting to and fro.

'Oh my word!' Bellingham sagged against the bench. 'Not again!'

'You were saying?' asked Cain coolly.

Viorica took the scissors which were lying at hand and cut the cat's limbs free of the constriction of its outer bandage. It rolled on to its stomach, stretched, then stood up and butted Mel in the stomach. Its bony, bandaged tail stuck up like a pole behind it.

'I was just exploring,' groaned Bellingham. 'I thought a cat would not harm anyone.' He grabbed a hammer. 'Now I'll have to destroy it.'

Cain gripped his wrist and wrestled the hammer from him. 'You will do no such thing. You've brought her back to life; now she has the right to her existence.'

Mel exchanged a wry glance with his reflection in

a mirror over the workbench. He rather thought *he* might have been responsible for reanimating the cat, completing the process Bellingham had begun. He stroked the cat, who arched under his palm.

Bellingham collapsed into a chair and took a swig of brandy from a pocket flask. 'Oh my days!'

'This is not the disaster you fear, professor,' said Cain. 'We can be trusted. We will even take care of the cat for you.'

'You will? Thank you, thank you, my boy!'

'All you need do in exchange is tell us who else has been looking into these and similar secrets. You must have noticed the new policy of the Chief Butler? He is terrorizing London by creating doubles that can suffer no harm – all of the consequences fall on the originals.'

'Indeed, it is an outrage.' Bellingham mopped his brow with a silk handkerchief.

'It looks to the uninformed like magic, but you and I both know that what appears to be magic has an explanation in science. As the Empire expands, the secret knowledge of the ancients is being uncovered by your fellow explorers. Who else is doing as you are – experimenting with these hitherto unknown powers?'

The cat jumped off the bench and tried to wind round the scientist's legs. Bellingham folded his knees and hugged them, keeping his feet off the floor. The cat returned to Mel in disgust.

While Cain waited the professor out, Viorica

wandered over to the mirror Mel had looked in. Her reflection did not appear, but Bellingham was too distracted to notice.

'There are many of us,' the scientist said at length. 'Your father was part of our group while he was alive. We formed a secret society – its members share our finds with each other to see who can be the first to unlock their mysteries. All of us scientists are united in our endeavour to probe the secret of life.'

Cain did not appear surprised to hear that his father had participated in such a group. 'And are any of Burlington's people in this society?'

Bellingham nodded, fear clouding his expression. 'You promise you will not tell?'

'I gave you my word that we can be trusted. Our purpose here is merely to arm ourselves with knowledge to fight the Chief Butler.'

Bellingham's eyes lit up with admiration. 'Your father would be proud of you. You are right to stand up to the Chief Butler. I have buried myself here, not wanting to see what has been happening outside but I knew – I knew.'

'Knew what?'

'Dorian Gray was the first. He was the one who specialized in doppelgängers – we all took our research to him. I believe he found the secret of a psychic ointment in an old herbal from Khartoum.'

'Psychic ointment?' asked Cain. Now they were getting somewhere.

'Yes. The ancient priests aspired to catch souls of the living in the walls of the tombs – servants who could attend their masters for all eternity.'

'Let me guess: if you mix this ointment with paint or use it as part of the developing process of a photographic plate, the same connection is established?'

Bellingham rocked in misery, eyes following the cat as she sniffed under his workbench. 'Yes, yes. As your likeness is taken, the filaments of your soul knit with the picture and the transfer begins.'

'Is the process reversible?' asked Mel.

'I don't know.'

'What's in this ointment?'

'I do not know exactly, but Gray has asked me for mummy dust on several occasions. Dust from the brain only.'

Cain scooped up the cat and cradled her in his arms. 'Remarkable.' Mel wasn't sure if he was talking about the ointment or the cat – or both. 'And the portraits where no living person is behind them – how can those be brought to life?'

Bellingham laced his fingers together, clasping his knees. 'I believe that they must be animated by connection with a living person, projections of his or her brain.' He looked away. 'Oh, I really shouldn't be telling you all this!'

Cain ignored the protest. 'How would that work?'

'Well, if I were doing it, I would paint over the image

with the ointment, building the connection. Only a very exceptional person could do this. If you are strong enough – dare I say wicked enough? – your soul could theoretically rip the picture from the frame and send it out in our three dimensional world, a puppet answerable to the master, held in being by strength of will.'

'Until it meets a greater force.' Cain's gaze slid to Mel.

'Indeed.'

Viorica picked up a monkey skull and tapped the cranium with her sharp nail. 'What about Burlington? Is he part of your circle?'

Bellingham cringed and closed his eyes.

'Come, come, professor: don't let us down now,' encouraged Cain. 'You say you felt guilty for shutting yourself away in here while he strengthens his grip on power. If you know something, you can do your bit by telling us.'

Bellingham took another swig from his flask. 'Burlington is no scientist. He really is – or was – a butler.'

A suspicion edged into Mel's mind. 'Who to?' he asked. 'Before the Queen, I mean?'

'To one called the Inventor.'

Mel's heart lurched. Viorica drew a sharp intake of breath.

'And who is that?' asked Mel.

'No one knows. He is very clever, very powerful; he is also continually on the move in that big ship of his. Voyages of exploration, he calls them, but I suspect he keeps out of society because he prefers to be his own master.'

'Have you seen him?' pressed Mel.

Cain passed the cat to Mel to stroke, a silent gesture of support.

'Once. He attended the Royal Society when I exhibited my finds five years ago. He sat in a private box to listen to my lecture and did not emerge from the shadows.'

'Is he English?'

Bellingham shrugged helplessly. 'I don't know what he is, other than he's very dangerous and undoubtedly the best mind of our generation. His published papers are wonders of experimental science.'

'His area is . . .?'

'There are so many. Electricity, electromagnetism, power generation, anatomy – and that is just the tip of the iceberg.'

'And Burlington was his butler?'

'Indeed. But when I saw Burlington first he did not look as he does in his statue in Trafalgar Square. Then, he was only a little over my height and thin – an inconsequential fellow. He has changed.'

'Or been changed,' concluded Cain. He bowed to the professor. 'Thank you for telling us this: you have been most helpful to our enquiries.'

Bellingham stood up, his hands fretting at his sides.

'I'm sorry I've not done more. You will not tell anyone what I said?'

'Naturally not.'

Bellingham showed them to the door. 'It was a . . . a pleasure meeting you, I think.' He shook hands with Mel and Cain and bowed to Viorica. 'Good luck. And don't let anyone see the cat!'

Mr Copperfield slumped in a corner, nursing a bloody nose. He had come off much better than the portrait duchess in white satin: she was ripped to pieces and strewn around the dining room, a hand flapping feebly, a slippered toe wriggling under the sideboard.

'Can you do nothing right? I ask you to find a solitary boy and you fail utterly. Instead he waltzes up to the Palace and explodes half my army!' roared Burlington. The government ministers quivered at the table, heads bowed so as not to attract attention. 'Pah! I am surrounded by idiots! You should be skinned and spitted over a fire for your incompetence.' The Chief Butler paced. Today he was wearing a long black robe, belted with a white silk rope. 'Bracknell, take charge of my valet, the Dr Foster double.'

Lady Bracknell's eyes flashed at the disrespect with which she had been addressed, but even she dared say nothing. 'Yes, sir,' she said tersely.

'Bring him to the National Gallery with the other captives. As all attempts to capture Melchizedek Foster have failed, I have no other option. I will make the boy come to me by torturing the Foster portrait.'

'Of course, sir.' Lady Bracknell rose. 'Shall I send for him now?'

'Go fetch him yourself. He is folding sheets in my chambers. I want no mistakes.'

Lady Bracknell swept out with an indignant twitch of her lavender skirt.

Burlington swung round with a flutter of black robe. 'Gray, how many people have you photographed?'

The elegant gentleman stood up, pink rosebud in his lapel. 'Ten thousand in the square, sir. But my assistant, Mr Wallace, had a suggestion about schools that will shorten our task. Most children are photographed each year in their classes. It is merely a question of sending out teams of photographers to all London schools. I've set some of my best people to do so.'

Burlington's fury ebbed at this news. 'Excellent work, Gray. Animate them immediately you receive the photographs and send the doubles out on the streets. The Resistance won't dare attack children. Copperfield?'

Mr Copperfield flinched. 'Yes, sir?'

'Have the newspapers tell the population that anyone sheltering Melchizedek Foster, or one of the rogue monsters, will have their image animated and punished. One or two doubles thrown on a bonfire will keep the rest in line.'

Mr Copperfield gulped. 'Yes, sir.'

'And it won't all be bad news.' Burlington wiped sweat from his brow and flicked it at his ministers. 'Tell them that the Queen will be attending the burning. We'll hold it in Trafalgar Square tomorrow morning. She will be looking her best, quite like her old self.' Burlington's eyes moved to the portrait over the fireplace of the Queen in her official robes. 'They will understand then that my actions have her blessing. Our new order should be welcomed by all loyal subjects.' Burlington smiled at his private secretary. 'Including you.'

Mr Copperfield forced himself to nod. 'Of course, sir.' He hurried out and immediately collapsed on a chair against the wall in the corridor. 'Oh, what the Dickens will come next?' he groaned. He mopped his brow with a white linen handkerchief stitched by his wife, who had died two years ago. What would Agatha say about this? She would be ashamed to find him serving such a beast.

And the Chief Butler was clearly planning to animate a picture of the Queen and use that as her replacement – if he had not done so already. The Queen had not been her old self ever since Burlington first took up his post as butler.

Mr Copperfield closed his eyes. 'No two ways about it, David,' he muttered to himself. 'That's treason, that is.'

Enough was enough. He might be but a worm to Burlington but he refused to be squashed under the

Chief Butler's heel any longer. His wife was not here to be hurt, his children were fortunately flourishing in lives far from the capital: if he could not afford to stand up to Burlington, who could?

But who would help him? The only candidates appeared to be Melchizedek Foster and the rogue monsters.

The Queen's Pomeranian sniffed at Mr Copperfield's shoes and whined. He looked down to see a fluffy face with dark black eyes gazing up at him.

'Well, Moppet,' said Mr Copperfield, getting wearily to his feet and scooping up the dog. 'I am leaving my post, and I think you'd better come with me. I'm not sure what would become of either of us if we stayed.' Mr Copperfield walked out of the Palace, aware that there were at least three pictures of him left behind somewhere in the vaults. Burlington was taking no chances with his own staff and had locked the pictures away as assurances of good behaviour. There was some comfort to be found in his late spark of courage, but the presiding emotion as he made his way to the Underground station was undoubtedly terror.

Chapter Fifteen
Copperfield's Deduction

The Monster Resistance were gathered around the table in the library leafing through catalogues of the Queen's paintings.

'We need to discover if Master Foster can destroy the double with no harm to the original,' announced Abel after Cain had recounted their meeting with the professor. He had assumed the elegant form and allowed Cain his turn as the rough one. Mel had realized that this latter was the shape they both preferred, finding the gentlemanly one too confining.

'I would still like to understand more about how his power works,' said Cain, rubbing his prickly chin in thought as he contemplated a print of an Italian landscape. 'I bet Burlington knows, or he would not be putting so much into finding Master Foster. It must be something to do with what the Inventor did.'

Mel was keeping very quiet. The new information they had learned about his father, the Inventor, had shaken him. He sounded even worse than Burlington.

Eve tried to nudge him discreetly; instead, she made him stumble. She steadied him with a hand on his elbow. 'Do not be troubled, Mel Foster,' she whispered. 'My father's making-father was a very poor specimen. You are not to blame for those who gave you life.'

The mummy came in with a cart of cake and tea, the cat strolling along happily at his heels. The Egyptian had been overjoyed to see his old pet and had been baking thank you cakes ever since. The meeting paused to allow tea to be served.

Viorica picked at the red icing on her slice of cake. The cochineal colouring, made from beetles' blood, was the only part she would eat. 'What we require is a safe test subject: an object that Burlington has animated and that we know still exists in the real world.'

'The Great Western Express?' suggested Abel, hand touching his ribs in memory of his close encounter. He sat down in a winged armchair and sipped his tea from a bone china cup with his little finger crooked.

'Already been broken up for scrap some years back,' replied Cain, shovelling sugar lumps into a mug of strong tea. 'If the boy did explode the original when he touched the copy, the only trace would be some dust in a scrapyard, impossible to identify. Besides it's a machine, not a living thing.'

'How about this?' asked Viorica, pointing to a painting of a giraffe in the catalogue. 'Do you think that is still alive?'

Mel wrinkled his nose. 'Even if it is, I don't want to experiment on animals.'

Three rapid knocks and a sharp bark broke the quiet of the house. Marley drifted to the entrance and stuck his head through the place where the knocker was fixed on the outside to see who it was.

'It is an elderly gentleman, sirs,' the ghost informed the Jekylls.

Cain raised a brow. 'Anyone expecting a caller?' No one replied. 'Then I had better send him on his way. Stay out of sight, all of you.' He strode into the hall and threw open the door. 'Get lost! We don't want anything you might be selling; our souls are fine, thank you; and no, I don't want to buy fire insurance!'

A little fluffball of a dog ran between Cain's legs.

'Mr Jekyll?' The caller's voice was shaky, recoiling from the hostility coming his way.

'What's it to you? And get your blasted dog out of my house!'

The Pomeranian was dancing in circles on the tiled floor, yapping hysterically. The raven decided that it would be good sport to dive at the creature, taking passing tugs at the pink bow on the top of its head until it unravelled.

'Stop it, Raven!' called Mel from behind the door in the library. 'Can't you see you're upsetting it!'

The Pomeranian was so overcome that it left a little puddle and then hid under the hat stand. It shook so hard the caps and bonnets tumbled around it like autumn apples.

'Look what your ridiculous pet just did!' growled Cain, as his favourite hat rolled into the wet patch.

'It's not my dog, sir,' replied the visitor, gathering some scraps of dignity.

'That poor excuse of a mutt certainly isn't mine.'

Mel heard the man give an offended gasp. 'Don't you insult Moppet, you scoundrel! That dog, I'll have you know, belongs to the Queen herself!'

The raven prepared itself for another flypast. Mel darted out of the library, picked up the dog and ran to the front door.

'Here, sir: take it.'

The old man on the step swayed, hand going to his forehead. He looked close to collapse. 'So this is the right house. Thank the lord!'

'I told you to stay hidden! Can't you ever follow orders?' grunted Cain. He heaved their visitor inside by his collar and slammed the door. 'You, sit there.' He shoved the gentleman on to the bench against the wall. 'Tell us what you mean about the "right house"? Who the blazes are you?'

'You're scaring him. Let me talk to him.' Mel put the Pomeranian on the old man's knee, thinking it would comfort him. 'Don't worry too much about Master Cain, sir; his bark is worse than his bite.'

The man smiled slightly. 'Thank you.'

'It's his brother who scares the life out of me.'

'By that he means me.' Abel came into view, his shirt open at the collar, cravat loose around his neck, completely at ease. 'Has Master Foster landed us in another mess, Cain?'

'Afraid so, brother.'

'We really must have a long talk about rules and penalties, Master Foster.'

'But not now,' grinned Mel. 'Your name, sir?'

The old man pushed the dog gently from his lap and stood up. He bowed with old-fashioned manners. 'David Copperfield at your service, sir. Private secretary to Her Majesty the Queen until eleven o'clock this morning.'

Mel glanced out of the window, gauging how much time has passed. 'Does anyone know you are here?'

'No. I promise you, I told no one.'

'That's a relief. Who do you think we are?'

The raven flew back into the library with a squawk.

'I think you are a house of . . . of unusual inhabitants,' Mr Copperfield said diplomatically. 'And you're Melchizedek.'

Uh-oh: his identity was out. 'How did you know who I am?'

'You are London's most wanted person. The description fits – and I saw you from afar at the Palace battle.' Mr Copperfield mopped his brow. 'Do you mind if I sit down again?'

Mel helped him to a seat. 'Why are you here, sir?'

'Bless me: have I not explained? I really am most out of sorts today. I want to join your side.'

'We have a side?' muttered Abel.

'Yes, yes, you in the Monster Resistance – that's what the papers are calling you. You are the only people standing up to that awful man Burlington. He is committing treason and no one stops him.' Mr Copperfield's eyes were bright with indignation. 'He is planning to burn the doubles of any who oppose him to keep the rest of the population in line. Can you imagine what that will be like? To experience the pain of burning and be unable to do anything about it! It would kill you!' Mr Copperfield shuddered.

Mel knelt beside the man's knee, quick to see this was a very real fear for the visitor. 'And you – have you left any pictures of yourself behind, sir?'

Mr Copperfield nodded miserably. 'Yes,

unfortunately. I have no doubt I will be the first on the bonfire when he realizes what I've done, but I don't care. I don't care.'

Mel could see that, on the contrary, Mr Copperfield did care very much. He was simply being brave about the prospect of hideous pain. 'We won't let it come to that. We'll stop him.'

Mr Copperfield shook his head sadly. 'You can't promise that. If Burlington has got so far into the heart of the kingdom that he has the Queen in his power, what can you do?'

The library door swung fully open and Eve came out. Mr Copperfield's eyes widened, but Mel gave him points for not fainting. He tried to get up.

'*Non*, *non*, stay seated, Monsieur Copperfield,' said Eve.

Viorica glided to stand beside Eve.

The elderly man looked increasingly flustered. 'My dear – ladies, I apologise for rudely bursting in on your home. Only my great need excuses my poor manners.'

The Pomeranian took one sniff at Viorica's skirts, yelped and ran to Eve for comfort. *Sensible dog*, Mel thought.

'How did you find us?' asked Eve, giving the dog's tummy a rub with her toe.

Mr Copperfield pointed behind her. 'It was him.'

They all turned to see the mummy, who patted his chest and shook his head vigorously, denying that he had betrayed them.

'Mummy!' growled Cain.

'He did not tell me, of course; I meant that I used him to track you down.'

'Explain,' snapped Abel, alarmed at the chink in their defences.

'As I said, I saw you all at the battle outside the Palace.'

'You were on the balcony with Burlington,' said Mel, remembering. 'You warned us about the train.'

'I tried, at least.' Mr Copperfield touched his puffy lip, still sore from a recent blow. 'I saw your most unusual choice of driver and noticed that he had a label around his neck, though I couldn't make out the number. Putting two and two together is one of my few good points. I realized that he must be a relic of the ancient civilization of Egypt, and the label suggested that at some point he had been part of an archaeological auction. From that deduction, the rest was simple. I have an old school friend in the museum – a chap by the name of Bellingham.'

Cain and Abel exchanged a look. Bellingham was their leak.

'I went to him, asking if he knew anyone who had bought an Egyptian mummy matching that description at auction. He was at first rather shocked that I had seen one of his finds walking about in daylight, but with so many more terrible things happening in London these days, I'm pleased to report that he recovered when I assured him his mummy was helping you fight Burlington. After giving my solemn word that my only wish was to aid you, he told me what I needed to know. Your address, sir, is listed in the museum's records from when you took delivery of the mummy.'

'Viorica, if you would be so kind?' said Abel in a low voice.

She nodded and went to the door. Mel guessed that a vampire bat would soon be visiting the museum archives to remove all trace of the Jekylls' purchase.

Mr Copperfield did not notice her leave. He was still admiring the mummy. 'If Bellingham had known of this splendid creature's particular animated properties before he auctioned him, I wager you would have had to pay much more than fifty guineas for him.'

The mummy threw his hands up in the air and stamped out through the servant's exit.

'What did I say?' asked Mr Copperfield in consternation.

'We told him we paid two hundred,' said Abel. 'Now he's upset.'

'I will go and console him,' said Eve. 'Come, *mon petit chien*. We will see what we can find for you in the kitchen.'

The dog trotted out at the giantess's heels.

Mr Copperfield wrung his hands briefly, then tucked them firmly in his pockets to prevent a repeat of the gesture. 'Bellingham said you were the only ones who could help me.'

'So you come here for sanctuary?' asked Mel.

Mr Copperfield shook his head, looking very sad. 'Not that, dear boy. My days are numbered, no matter what you do for me. No, I come here with information. I am party to things you need to know if you are going to defeat this fiend.'

'What do you think?' Mel asked the twins.

Cain and Abel exchanged a long look. Cain nodded. 'I'll get the mop.' He looked up at the bird who had taken a new perch on the bannister on the floor above. 'Raven, stop scaring the dog, or next time I'll use your feathers to clear up.'

With that, the twins signalled that they had accepted their new guests.

After the mummy served tea in the library, Mel and Eve took their new guest upstairs to see Dr Foster so he could witness first-hand the effect of the Chief Butler's picture transfer. They found Inky and Nightie looking after the slumbering patient, reading him nursery rhymes – the fairies' choice, Mel suspected.

'Mel Foster has the power to wake people up, like he woke me from ice,' Eve explained.

'Indeed?' marvelled Mr Copperfield.

'And he can even wake up those who have had their energy stolen by doubles. Go on, Mel Foster: show Monsieur Copperfield.'

Mel gently touched Dr Foster's hand and the old gentleman roused from his sleep.

'W-what's this?' he gasped, stuttering awake.

Mr Copperfield bowed. 'My name's Copperfield. Apologies for disturbing you, sir. We wished to ask how you are feeling?'

Dr Foster sighed and settled back on the pillow. 'Stretched and pummelled like bread dough.'

'But at the moment?' asked Mr Copperfield carefully. 'Nothing particularly painful?'

'No. Thanks to these charming creatures,' Dr Foster gestured to the attentive fairies, 'I've had splendid dreams of cockleshell gardens and lambs.'

Inky and Nightie beamed.

But Dr Foster was no fool. His gaze sharpened. 'What do you know, sir, about my condition?'

Hesitating a second, Mr Copperfield dug in his pocket and pulled out a folded sheet of paper. He flattened it out. 'The Chief Butler has had this poster prepared.'

Melchizedek Foster!

SURRENDER IMMEDIATELY

TO A MEMBER OF THE

MONSTER PATROL

or **DR FOSTER** will be punished in your place

by order of
H.M. The Queen

'I took this as I left the Palace. It is going up all over London,' explained Mr Copperfield.

'Thunder and lightning!' gasped Dr Foster, patting himself nervously.

'He means to trap the lad.'

Dr Foster reached for Mel. 'Melchizedek, you must at all costs stay out of his grasp.'

All costs? wondered Mel. Even at the cost of his old guardian's life?

'What will this villain do to the double?' asked Eve in horror.

Mr Copperfield winced. 'I believe Burlington plans to torture him at a burning ceremony in Trafalgar Square.'

'*Diable*!'

Indeed, Burlington was a devil. Mel clenched his fists, wishing he could zap the Chief Butler with a bolt of power and put an end to him. 'If only I could break this link between you and your portrait, sir, then we wouldn't need to worry.'

Dr Foster frowned. 'What would happen to me if you did away with my picture, like you did the others you have touched?'

'I don't know!' groaned Mel. 'It might free you, but it might kill you. The ones I've destroyed so far have been of people and things long gone, not a living man.'

Dr Foster closed his eyes for a moment and took

a deep breath. 'Then you must use me, my boy. Your powers are needed to destroy Burlington's armies, but you can't touch any doubles of real people until you know the result. Let me make the sacrifice of being your test subject.'

Mel reared back. 'No, I can't.'

'I'm old – worn out.' Dr Foster wryly showed them the flaky patch on his arm where the canvas was showing through. 'Better me than some innocent schoolchild whose picture has been misused.'

'He is right,' said Eve, tears glinting in her mismatched eyes but her expression fierce. 'Dr Foster is a man of great courage: you should accept his offer.'

Mel didn't want to do any such thing, but he could see that it was the surest way of finding out the extent of his gift.

'My dear lady,' said Mr Copperfield, 'I am glad you agree, but just how is young Melchizedek going to get close enough to the double to make this experiment?'

'It's plain as a pikestaff,' came a gruff voice from the doorway. 'The Dr Foster double is with the Chief Butler.'

Mel looked round to find the twins had been listening in. It was Cain who had spoken.

'So we hand the boy over to Burlington,' finished Abel.

Mr Copperfield put his head in his hands. Eve was too shocked to speak.

'But I thought the plan was to keep me away from him at all costs?' Mel had much preferred that idea, as it was less likely to result in a painful death.

'Not *at all costs*, no,' said Cain, wiping his nose on a cuff. 'Only as long as it was the best course of action. Now it isn't.'

Eve was breathing heavily, a lioness on the verge of a roar.

'But . . .!' began Mel.

'No buts, Master Foster,' said Abel severely. 'Are you part of our resistance or not?'

Mel nodded, wondering if he had been wrong to think promotion from third footman a good thing.

'Then you must trust us. We can't wait for the information to fall into our laps; we have to shake it down from the tree.'

Eve seized Abel's arm and span him to face her. She lifted him up so his feet kicked free of the floor. 'Mel Foster is our only chance of beating the Chief Butler! You do not hand over the king in a game of chess, *comprenez*?'

'Hardly a king. I'd say Master Foster was more a very useful knight or bishop.' Cain smiled wryly. 'And please, put my brother down.'

One eye swivelled in his direction. '*Non*. But you

are next if you hurt him.'

Mel tugged Eve's elbow. 'Look, let's just think about this for a moment.'

Abel kicked out ineffectually. 'No, we can't. Put me down.'

Eve growled. Cain took a step forward.

'Please, Eve,' said Mel in a low voice.

Abel dropped free from Eve's grip.

'There is no time left.' Abel brushed off the sleeves of his jacket. 'As Mr Copperfield has told us, tomorrow Burlington is going to start burning doubles. The bonfire in Trafalgar Square will mark the end of British civilization and the start of the same doubling process in all countries across the world where paintings or photographs exist.'

'No government will be safe,' said Cain. 'There will be nothing beyond Burlington's reach, no ruler he can't topple. This has to be the aim of his plan – or the plan of his master, the Inventor.'

'But if Master Foster can get close enough to explode my double,' the poor doctor flinched at Abel's vivid description, 'we will be able to tell if we have a power that we can use against Burlington's army.'

'And if he kills Mel Foster on sight, what then?' asked Eve, spitting out the words. 'What becomes of your most wonderful plan?'

'I very much doubt he will.' Cain thumped her on

the back, then shook his hand in the air with a grimace at her unyielding flesh. 'As Mel is the Inventor's son, Burlington will think twice before striking him down on the spot. It is more likely there are other plans for him.'

'You suppose a great deal,' snarled Eve.

'Don't get all steamed up, mademoiselle,' said Cain, 'we are not intending to leave Mel alone in the lion's den.'

'And he has said he wants to deal with the boy himself,' conceded Mr Copperfield. 'He has ordered that no one is to harm him.'

'Mr Copperfield, I fear we must ask you and the dog to go back to the Palace,' said Abel solemnly.

The elderly man went pale. 'You must?'

'Indeed. For two reasons: first, we would spare you the pain of any reprisal against you. If you go back now, it is possible no one will know you have changed allegiance.'

Mr Copperfield rubbed the thighs of his black trousers nervously. 'True.'

'Secondly, you are far more useful to us on the inside.'

'If Mr Copperfield will forgive me for saying so,' said Eve, 'I do not think his presence will be enough to stop Burlington killing Mel Foster, if that is his plan.'

'Nothing to forgive, mademoiselle: you're quite right,' agreed Mr Copperfield.

'This is too dangerous,' concluded Eve.

Abel turned to her. 'Everything is dangerous, mademoiselle; but most dangerous of all is doing nothing.'

'And we'll be closer to Mel than you think,' said Cain. 'You see, I'm going to be the one to turn the boy in. As a loyal junior officer in the Monster Patrol, I will insist on seeing him all the way to the Chief Butler himself. I promise you that they will have to kill me first before they harm Mel.'

'And if they do kill you?' asked Eve bluntly, folding her arms.

'Then I suppose it won't matter to me after that, will it?' Cain flashed one of his reckless grins at Mel. 'You agree to this, Mel?'

Mel gulped. It was the first time Cain had called him by his first name, a sure sign he was being manipulated in a friendly fashion. He was not stupid – he didn't want to do this at all – but with so many people prepared to put their lives on the line to save Queen and country, how could he say no?

'I'll do it.'

Eve gave a sigh like the cracking of a great iceberg.

Mel was jolted from his gloomy thoughts by Inky and Nightie, who jumped up on the bedhead behind Dr Foster and began pointing at their chests.

Mel remembered his promise to the fairies. 'Could

Incubus and Nightmare come with me? They are good at slipping into places without being seen.'

Cain adjusted the knotted handkerchief at his neck. 'I'm not too happy with that. They're just little chaps.'

Inky blew a raspberry.

Abel studied his manicured fingernails. 'Little, but useful. They may go, but on one condition: they'll have to wear masks.'

'Hurrah!' squeaked Nightie, turning a complete somersault and landing in the chamber pot.

Chapter Sixteen
Trafalgar Burning

After a night prowl, Viorica reported that although Londoners were muttering together over their beers about the poor kid who had attracted the Chief Butler's ire, everyone was too scared to do anything about it. Mr Copperfield was right: there was no one else left who was able to stop him. Burlington had moved so quickly that even the usually lively Cockney crowd were reluctant to rebel. Legions of false schoolchildren, all dressed in their smartest clothes for their class pictures, were already patrolling the streets, and parents were too afraid to act in case their real sons and daughters suffered for it. The net was tightening: any boy of Mel's age caught outside was checked for a burn mark on his chest. Families were staying indoors and the streets were unnaturally quiet – apart, that was, from the rustle of unsmiling photographic children silently walking their beats.

At the back exit to the house, Cain tied Mel's wrists loosely behind his back. 'Give a tug and that knot will come free,' he promised. 'I've persuaded Abel to delay changing shape a day so I have the strength to fight should I need it.'

'That's good,' said Mel hollowly.

'Besides, our gentlemanly identity is too well known in society to get through to the Chief Butler without being recognized. We've always kept this one for the dodgy work. We don't want the Monster Patrol banging on our door later today if we have to flee back here. Not that I don't think we'll be triumphant.' Cain said it with such grim humour that Mel didn't believe he thought that at all.

Mel wished he could put on his uniform and mask, but of course that was completely out of the question. 'You're really sure about this?'

'About fifty-fifty.' Cain tugged a helmet over his wiry hair. He had 'borrowed' a Monster Patrol uniform off a man Viorica had brought home for dinner. The Patrolman was now lying unconscious, short of a pint of blood and tied up in the cellar but otherwise unharmed.

'Those odds aren't good.'

'It could be worse: I could've told you the truth.'

'And what is the truth?'

'The real odds are somewhere in the low teens. That's what comes of being desperate. This scheme is our last throw of the dice to win this game against the Chief Butler.'

'You really have a gift for comfort, don't you?'

'I'm the nice brother, remember?'

Mel gave a choked laugh. 'Maybe I'm changing my mind about that.'

'Ready?' asked Abel, opening the door to the stable where their vehicles were stored. He was going to drive the horse-drawn carriage, with Mel inside it, to the National Gallery. This building had become the central prison of the Burlington regime since the doubles programme had been started. The mummy was to follow a few minutes later in the horseless carriage. He was to bring Dr Foster as close to Trafalgar Square as he could. That way the raven would be able to report the result – happy or disastrous – of Mel's touching Foster's double in time to make a difference to the anticipated battle.

Unfortunately, the mummy's part in the plan had had to be negotiated by Eve – he was still not talking to the twins. Not that he talked anyway, Mel corrected himself, but now he wasn't even drawing hieroglyphics for them – except one very rude one that Eve wouldn't show Mel.

'It's going to take a very expensive sarcophagus for him to sleep in before he forgives us,' sighed Cain as the mummy ostentatiously turned his back on him and wiped the windscreen with a loose bandage. 'Lots of gold leaf.'

The cat turned her rear to Abel and flicked a dismissive tail in his general direction. She wound round Mel's ankles with a rasp of wrapped sides that replaced a purr, then leapt up on the rear seat next to the blanket-swaddled Dr Foster.

'Do what you must, Melchizedek, and don't worry about me!' called the doctor.

'All aboard, *mesdames*, *messieurs*!' Eve got inside the carriage, making the springs creak. Viorica transformed into mist, taking the form of a bat to hang from the roof. Cain sat opposite as Mel squeezed on the seat next to Eve. The two monster fairies settled in the capacious pockets of Cain's coat, heads peeking out like joeys in a kangaroo's pouch. Abel clicked his tongue and the horse trotted out of the stable in the mews, Mr Marley closing the gate behind them.

'Let's run through the plan again,' said Cain as the streets of London jogged past the window. 'By now, Mr Copperfield should be back with Burlington. We know that the Chief Butler is making an appearance this morning with his fake Queen and Dr Foster's double at the burning ceremony outside the National Gallery. Mel appearing there should at least delay Burlington's plans for incinerating anyone, as he'll want to deal with him first. I'll insist on my reward so he takes us inside together. That's when Mel touches the Foster double.'

Mel stared glumly at his scuffed shoes. Cain nudged him. 'You remember the rest?'

'Yes: we delay Burlington until the raven reports the result of the test, and then I either destroy the rest of the doubles of real people or get clear of them if it's dangerous to touch them. Meanwhile you free the prisoners in the gallery cells, to even out the odds if it comes to a battle. This all seems a bit woolly to me.'

'Can't be helped, Mel. Resistance fighters never stick to plans – we aren't in control of the conditions on the battlefield.'

'And if I can't delay him any longer – or he tries to kill me?'

'You escape with the help of the fairies and Mr Copperfield and make a run for it. We'll be waiting for you, fighting every inch of the way.'

'We'll sneak in like ninjas,' squeaked Inky.

'Right behind you!' agreed Nightie.

'I do not like this,' muttered Eve. 'I want to be with Mel Foster.'

Cain shook his head. 'Nah, not possible. We can't think of a way to disguise you. You'll have to trust the fairies and Viorica to go first. You follow when the fight gets going.'

The idea was for the vampire to follow Mel and Cain in bat form and relay any distress calls to the rest of the team waiting in the carriage.

Mel closed his eyes, seeking some privacy to gather his courage. He reminded himself that he would at the very least be sparing some innocents from a bonfire and honouring Dr Foster's sacrifice.

The carriage passed the theatres on Shaftesbury Avenue. Cain was drilling the fairies and Viorica in their roles, leaving Mel and Eve to talk privately.

'You know, Eve, I think a little part of me wants to meet the Chief Butler,' Mel admitted. 'It's like he's a magnet and I'm an iron filing.'

'I want to meet him too – to kick him out of London by his, how do you call it in English?' She pointed behind her and waggled her eyebrows.

Mel laughed, knowing she was trying to cheer him up. 'There are many words. I'll tell you later. But don't you think it's amazing how quickly Burlington overthrew the government?'

'Our enemy is a very dangerous man. And do not forget he has this link to the Inventor.'

'My father.' Mel shivered.

'An even more dangerous man.'

Mel let his weight rest against her arm, seeking comfort. 'I'm worried that this is a huge mistake. The twins' plan leaves too much to chance.'

She frowned. 'You know I'm against it.'

'I think I have to try, but I'm worried that the twins believe they're the ones setting a trap; what if it's really the other way round?'

'I fear that too.' She put her arm around him, remembering to keep her squeeze delicate this time. 'You are very brave to do this, Mel Foster.'

It wasn't bravery, thought Mel. If he had any sense, he would be jumping out of the carriage and running for the hills, but something kept him nailed to the spot. It wasn't courage, or any of the other qualities heroes were supposed to have – it was because he did not want to disappoint his friends.

The carriage was making slow progress down St Martin's Lane. Cain stuck his head out of the window.

'Crowds already gathering,' he reported. 'And I thought all that had gone when they banned public executions.'

'That is probably why Burlington is popular in some quarters,' suggested Viorica. 'He knows how to appeal to the bloodthirsty mob.'

Abel pulled up the horse at the steps of St Martin-in-the-Fields. Despite its name, the church was no longer among fields, but in the paved acre of Trafalgar Square. From the steps they had a clear view right across the plaza with its encircling pale stone buildings, all pillared and polished. This was formal, ceremonial London: a space for public protest and display. Daunted, Mel concentrated on breathing rather than thinking. He couldn't afford to lose his nerve now.

'What's going on?' Mel asked Cain, who had the best view.

'There's a platform outside the National Gallery and a ramp leading to the empty statue plinth. That's been piled with wood for the bonfire.'

The sound of marching feet echoed through the narrow streets around Trafalgar Square. Rank upon rank of Monster Patrolmen poured into the square from all corners. Many in the crowd waved little red and black flags to greet them. The huge black-bronze lions at the foot of the column gazed on blankly. Mel traced the stone pillar upwards. At the top was a bare-chested statue of Burlington in flowing robes, glamorous, powerful and dangerous.

The doors to the National Gallery opened and the main players in this scene emerged. First came Lady Bracknell and her lieutenant Mr Squeers, then a squad of soldiers. They lined the ramp to the bonfire, Lady Bracknell standing ready with a taper to light the fire. Behind her came the prisoners, three men and a woman, their doubles each walking in step with the original. Then came the familiar figure of the portrait Dr Foster, tapping his umbrella jauntily as he waved to the crowd. At the rear of the procession came the Chief Butler, escorting the Queen in her robes of state. The people cheered her appearance lustily, relieved to have what they thought was proof that she was alive and well. The fake Victoria looked like a miniature galleon with black sails gliding to her berth. With a courtly bow, Burlington guided her to a throne under a canopy at the front of the staging. Once Victoria was seated, Burlington stepped forward and held up his hand for silence. He lifted a megaphone to his mouth.

'Subjects of Her Imperial Highness, you are here today to witness the punishment of those who have not obeyed her wishes.'

Now that he had demonstrated he had royal approval, Burlington had most of the crowd on his side. They hissed at the traitors.

'First, Inspector Bucket, late of the police force, who refused to transfer to the Monster Patrol.'

Boos and catcalls came from the most eager down the front as a lanky man in a grey suit was pushed forward. He gazed at the mockers in disdain. Others in the crowd murmured uneasily, but they were shouted down by the pro-Butler faction.

'Professor Pesca, Italian teacher, who wrote a letter of protest to *The Times* complaining about the abolition of Parliament.'

The little figure of the teacher stood proudly alongside the inspector, his white hair and bald spot gleaming in the sunshine.

'And finally, Mr and Mrs Jonathan Harker, who have tried to organize a private army to stand against me – I mean, the *Queen*.'

A young couple were shoved to the front, the man with his arm around his pretty wife. He was dark, she was fair, and both looked well-to-do. The husband wiped away the lady's tears, whispering encouragement. Their doubles mimicked their movements but their faces were blank of emotion, no more connection showing between them than strangers on the Underground.

Burlington clicked his fingers. 'Light the bonfire!'

Lady Bracknell put her taper to the kindling; flames leapt into the air, eating up the dry wood.

Burlington gestured to the blaze. 'There is another person who should be standing here.' Silence fell in the square, broken only by the flutter of flags and the crackle of flames. 'Yes, there is. The renegade, Melchizedek Foster – you've all seen the posters – he should have taken his place up here with the other traitors, but he has not given himself up. As a foretaste of the punishment to come, and as encouragement to Melchizedek Foster to do the decent thing, we are going to burn the right arm of the man who has stood as a father to him since his birth. Let that be a warning to you all: those who stretch out a hand to help one of the Queen's enemies shall have that limb cut off and thrown into the flames.'

Many in the crowd gasped in horror, but others cheered. The punishment, however, came as news to the doctor's double. As the Monster Patrolmen converged on him to rip off his arm, he woke up to the danger with a squawk, raced for the building and disappeared inside.

'The double's getting away. I think this would be a good moment.' Cain opened the door of the cab and dropped down to the ground. 'Come on, Mel.'

Mel smiled bravely at Eve, nodded to Viorica and followed Cain outside.

'*Bon chance, mon frère*,' whispered Eve.

As the screeching double of Dr Foster was caught and dragged back to the rostrum, Cain shouldered his way through the crowds, pulling Mel along with him.

'Make way!' he shouted. 'Clear a path there!'

People at first resisted but a whisper ran ahead. *It's the boy! It's him!* Like those fearing to catch a contagion, they fell back, leaving the way open.

Burlington hadn't noticed: he was giving orders to two of his biggest men to twist off the doctor's right arm. The painting double had fainted in fear.

'Oi! Sir! Chief Butler! I've got something for you! I've got the boy!' bellowed Cain.

Spinning to locate the voice, Burlington shouted, 'Is that him? Is that Melchizedek Foster?'

'I reckon so, sir. Leastways, I'm here to claim the reward, so I would be much obliged if you checked his identity.'

Burlington clapped his hands, raw jubilation coursing through him. 'Bring him up here.'

Cain shoved Mel along. They climbed up the steps to the platform. Mel noticed out of the corner of his eye that the Foster double was now lying stretched out at the fake Queen's feet.

Burlington stamped forward, every step making the boards judder. He seemed heavier than his size, like his limbs were made of a substance more weighty than flesh. He was decked out in black leather, gloves, boots and a whip stuck through his belt. Swooping down on his prey, he gripped Mel's hair and wrenched his head back. Hot garlic-laden breath puffed in Mel's face. He tugged the neck of Mel's shirt down to reveal the key-shaped scorch mark. Then he pulled a gold chain from around his own neck. A key dangled at the end – ordinary iron with a circular fob. He placed it against Mel's scar.

'A perfect match, Melchizedek.'

Mel raised his gaze to meet the eyes of his enemy. It felt as though everyone else had disappeared and he was falling into a dark night where only two red lamps shone. He swallowed, throat dry. Then Burlington abruptly released his grip and turned away, hands on hips, muscles in his back quivering like a racehorse that had just finished the Derby.

'Is it him, sir?' asked Cain.

Burlington strode back to face Mel. 'It is.' He pulled his whip from his waistband and twirled the leather stock in his hands.

Lady Bracknell approached him cautiously. 'Sir, the crowd is waiting.'

Burlington gestured her back irritably with a crack of his whip. 'Let them wait. The Queen has decided to delay the exhibition until noon. Isn't that right, Your Majesty?'

The counterfeit Queen rose and waved to the crowd, arm moving to and fro like a metronome.

'That'll do, Vicky,' snapped Burlington. 'Guards, put the prisoners back in their cells. You, Patrolman, bring the boy and follow me.'

'So far, so good,' muttered Cain. 'Just get close enough to the double.'

'Easier said than done,' Mel hissed at him. He watched for his chance, but the execution squad had already picked up the Foster double like a rolled rug and marched him back inside the National Gallery.

Once through the main doors, Queen Victoria walked into the cupboard in which visitors left their umbrellas and parcels. She sat down there to wait until she was required. The Foster double was dumped on a bench in the foyer.

Burlington swept on through the vast entrance hall with Mel and Cain. Mel could hear cries, howls and shouts from the rooms on either side. Many political objectors and monsters who had refused to join Burlington had been imprisoned here, kept in line by threats to their portrait doubles.

'So who are you, patrolman?' asked Burlington, throwing the remark over his shoulder to Cain.

'Constable Hyde, sir,' said Cain, glancing over his shoulder to check on Foster's double. It was still stretched out unconscious and they were getting further and further away from it.

'Where did you find the boy?'

Cain scratched his jaw. 'To be honest, Chief Butler, sir, he just handed himself over to me while I was on patrol.'

'I'll see that you are rewarded.' They had arrived at an entrance marked *The Queen's Private Collection*. Burlington kicked open the door and strode into a bright semicircular room, hung with pictures of the royal family and personal mementoes: hunting trophies and gifts from foreign rulers. A glass-domed roof bathed the room in light. An artist's easel stood to one side, a pot of oil on its ledge. From the acrid throat-choking smell, Mel thought that it had to be the mummy-dust concoction that brought pictures to life.

'Hyde, leave us now and report to Mr Gray in the photographic studio,' barked Burlington.

Cain shuffled, turning his helmet over and over in his hands. 'I was just doing my duty, sir. Now I come to think of it, I don't want no reward.'

Burlington took a whaling harpoon from the wall, leaving a blank above the brass plate engraved with *The weapon that killed Moby Dick*. He sat on a gilded chair with a red velvet seat that had been placed in the centre of the room. His sharp nails tapped on the harpoon pole. 'I insist. Bracknell, escort Constable Hyde to see Mr Gray.'

Cain glanced once at Mel. 'Much obliged, sir.' He tugged his forelock and followed the lady, passing

Mr Copperfield who slipped in through the same door. In the flurry of coming and going, the two fairies dropped out of Cain's pockets and sneaked along the skirting board, behind the boots of the Patrolmen who stood on guard along the walls.

Mel swallowed. Their plan was already going far off the rails.

Burlington seemed content for the moment just to study Mel. Not wanting to meet the Chief Butler's gaze, Mel examined the pictures instead. Every family group was missing one important figure: the Queen's consort.

Burlington gestured to the pot of oil. 'Miraculous invention, is it not? Painting brought to life.'

Mel said nothing.

Burlington caressed the harpoon. 'Do you know what I promised the Queen for her cooperation?'

Mel shook his head.

'Prince Albert, her much mourned husband. I told her I could bring him back from the dead.' Burlington smiled. 'Not the full truth, of course, as I can only return a copy, but you'd be surprised how satisfied she was by that.'

That was horrid, thought Mel: *using a grieving old lady's weakness*. Just one more bad thing to add to the pile of Burlington's sins.

'No,' mused Burlington, holding up the key and letting it spin on its chain, 'only you could have brought him back to *life* – under the right experimental conditions, naturally.'

'I could?' Despite his resolution to keep silent, Mel was surprised into speaking.

Burlington looked round the room at his honour guard. 'Leave us.'

With a click of their heels, the Patrolmen marched out in formation. Their faces were so hardened and lacking any sign of humanity that Mel could not tell if they were real people or doubles.

Mr Copperfield hesitated. 'I'll wait just outside the door, sir,' he said, more for Mel's benefit than the butler's.

'See how Gray is doing with that patrolman, Copperfield.' Burlington had not taken his eyes from Mel. 'I didn't like him. His loyalty must be pinned down.'

The fairies scurried under a cabinet of stuffed animals.

High overhead a bat flapped at the skylight, looking for a way inside. Wire, stretched across to deter pigeons, prevented her entering.

Mel's heart sank. They hadn't anticipated that barrier. Mel was down to only two monster fairies as his back up, and the Foster double was far out of reach. He didn't need the ghost of Jacob Marley to tell him he was doomed.

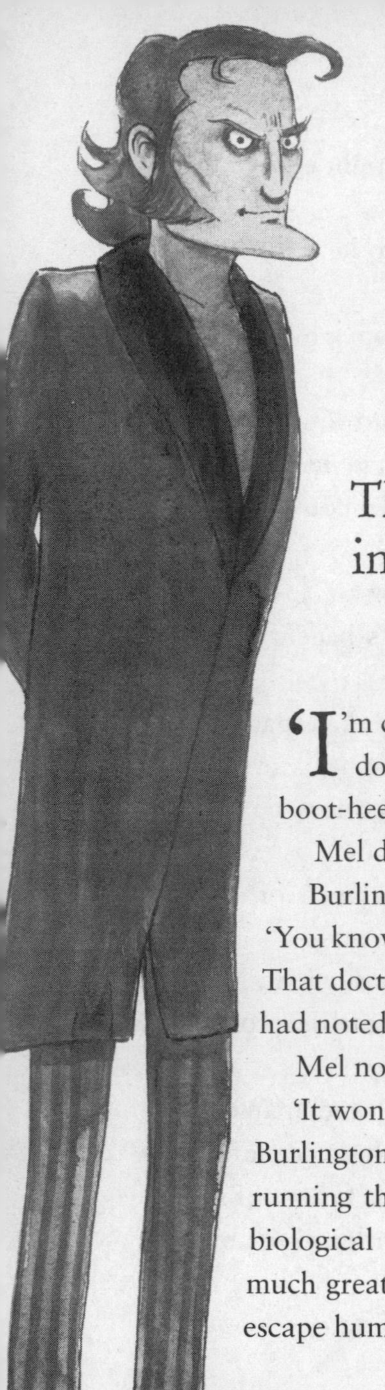

Chapter Seventeen

There Are More Things in Heaven and Earth . . .

'I'm curious: What do you think I should do with you?' Burlington tapped his boot-heel with his harpoon.

Mel dug his nails into his palms.

Burlington cocked his head to one side. 'You know now who your father is, I suppose? That doctor will have told you the rumour. He had noted it on your file.'

Mel nodded.

'It won't help you. The Inventor is not . . .' Burlington licked his lips, a slight shiver running through his body, 'interested in such biological mistakes. His goal is something much greater than that. His work will one day escape human limitations entirely.'

Mel had to ask. 'What work is that?'

Burlington fixed him with his gaze, waiting for something.

'Sir,' Mel added reluctantly.

'You see the first fruits before you.' Burlington gestured to his own bronzed chest and powerful limbs. 'Once I was no more than an ordinary man – weak, easily hurt, mortal; now I am as perfect as a human can be.'

Mel's tongue got there before his brain. 'So there was no cure for vanity, then?'

Burlington lashed out and struck Mel across the face.

'Next time you cheek me, I'll cut out your tongue!'

Mel believed him. He attempted to sound more humble. 'What are you going to do with me, sir?'

Burlington leaned the harpoon against the arm of his chair. 'I'm trying to decide. The Inventor wants you, dead or alive: he's not too fussed.'

Mel fought down his fear. Things had gone wrong, so now he needed to delay for as long as possible and pray for rescue. 'Why kill me? What threat could I possibly be?'

In answer, Burlington pulled out the key.

Mel shook his head: that couldn't be it. 'If the key opens something important, you've already got it.'

Burlington threw back his head and laughed. 'The key itself does not matter; it is what it did to you. Don't you know anything about it?' He let it sway like a hypnotist's pendulum. 'This key is famous. It was first used by Benjamin Franklin to draw lightning from the clouds. An admirer of that great American, the Inventor acquired it at auction and used it for his own work. He converted it to be able to trap the life force that inhabits all living things. He experimented on scores of people and discovered that when used with the right equipment it can suck all the energy from a body – every last flicker in nerve cell and muscle – energy that can be stored and reused.'

Mel suspected he was facing someone who had benefitted from that stored energy. If his guess was correct, Burlington had been pumped up from weakling to prime specimen at other people's expense. He thought of a question. 'What did it do to me? Clearly it didn't steal my life force or transform me – I'm still here.'

Burlington held the key loop to his eye, studying it carelessly. 'It malfunctioned.'

'I don't understand.'

'Your desperate fool of a mother gave birth to you on the road to Gloucester during a thunderstorm. The first thing she did was to put the key round your neck for safekeeping, knowing that your father considered it vital. Her little mind thought she was securing your inheritance, the key to a locked chest full of gold or something similar. But, exposed as you both were to the storm, the key attracted lightning and you were struck. The key released its stores of energy into the thing it was touching.'

'Me,' whispered Mel, rubbing his chest.

'It supercharged rather than transformed you – in a sense *you* became the key, holding the energy in its place.' Burlington let the key fall back on its chain. 'It is useless now – empty of power. I will return it to the Inventor only because he values its history.'

'But what about me?'

'I'll send you to him along with it for his experiments.' Burlington gave Mel an exulting smile. 'Pickled in a jar or locked in a cage, he doesn't mind which.'

Why was no one rescuing him? 'But . . . but why come for me now, after all these years?' Mel asked, desperately trying to buy more time.

Burlington waved the question off. 'Not through any great change of heart on his part. He knew you existed, of course, because of the enquiries Dr Foster made about your father, but he didn't expect you to survive the orphanage. Indeed, he gave you little thought until recently.'

It would have been better if the Inventor had gone on not thinking about him, decided Mel.

'He asked me to discover if you still lived when I came to London. You did, but that blasted Bracknell woman had unbeknown to us already sent you to sea.'

'Why did it matter if I was alive or not then?'

'Ah.' Burlington twirled the harpoon. 'He warned me that, theoretically, you could upset our plans due to the unfortunate side effects of the lightning strike.'

'Side effects?'

'Your ability to blast psychic creations with undiluted life force. You fry the connection between creator and double – surely you realize that? Now, this is all very touching, this talk of fathers and sons, but time is pressing. I have an empire to conquer,' he stood up and leaned the harpoon on his chair, 'for the Inventor.'

Mel tried to stall him once again. 'Why for him and not for yourself?'

'Simple, my dear doomed boy: he gives me life. You and I have that much in common.'

Seeing he was unable to do anything for Melchizedek at present, Mr Copperfield decided that his best course of action was to obey the Chief Butler's order. Cain had been taken to the photography studio next door, so Mr Copperfield followed.

'Hold still, lad,' said the guard responsible for getting the subjects into the head brace. 'Mr Gray has said you're to be photographed.'

Cain was trying to squirm free. 'Look, pal, I ain't one for this photography lark. Against my religion. It steals your soul.'

'There ain't no religion here but the one the Chief Butler approves. Everyone is to be photographed.'

Mr Wallace appeared from under the black hood of the camera, his brand standing out starkly on his cheek. 'Darwin's tortoise, Bates, how long is it going to take you to get the subject to keep still?'

'Right away, Mr Wallace.'

Mr Copperfield edged into the room as Bates and Cain struggled. They were about a match in muscles, but the twin stood no chance when two other Patrolmen joined the scrum. Cain was carried to the chair, hands locked to its arms, neck caught in the brace so he could not move his head. No use in a trial of strength, Mr Copperfield planned his more subtle move: he would let the photographic plate be taken, then act.

'Now, hold still. This won't hurt. Twenty seconds – that's all.' The photographer disappeared under the hood, his voice now muffled. 'One, two . . .'

Mr Copperfield rubbed his eyes: something very bizarre was happening to Cain Jekyll. His face appeared to be melting. Not just his face, his whole body was shifting, bones shortening, hair receding, limbs losing muscle.

'What the blue blazes is this?' exclaimed Bates.

'Nineteen, twenty.' Wallace came out from under the hood to face a completely different young man. Cain had turned into his brother, the elegant one with the supercilious smile. Arms thinner, he slid them out of the straps and stood up, clothes hanging loosely on his new slighter frame.

'Good luck with making anything of that picture, old bean,' Cain said with the poise of an educated young gentleman.

'But you . . .' spluttered Bates. 'What the . . .?'

'Old magic trick. Now, excuse me: I have business elsewhere. Mr Copperfield, if you would be so kind?'

Shaking off his dismay, Mr Copperfield hurried forward. 'Sir? Mr Abel?'

'No, I'm still Cain. Please conduct me to the cells.'

'Just a moment, sir: there is something I must do first.'

Fortunately, Mr Wallace was slow to realize that the private secretary had changed sides. 'Did you see that, Copperfield?' He lifted out the plate he had taken. 'I wonder how this will turn out? There might be a paper in it for the Royal Society!'

'Excuse me.' Mr Copperfield spoke so politely Wallace did not see it coming. The secretary took the plate and dropped it on the ground. It shattered. Then he picked up the box of exposed plates, Wallace's morning's work, and upended it so all the pieces smashed and mingled, impossible to reassemble in any order.

'Inspired thought, Mr Copperfield,' said Cain. 'Allow me.' He kicked over the camera, then tugged off the lens. 'Some weapons have to be put beyond use.' He lobbed the lens at the wall where the glass shivered into bits. 'To the cells, please.'

Patrolman Bates blocked the door. 'I don't how you did what you did, but magician or not, you're not leaving here.' He gestured to his allies to back him up.

'Oh dear, fisticuffs. I do prefer the other body for

that.' Cain rolled up his sleeves and beckoned Bates with his fingers, a mocking 'come closer' gesture.

Bates grinned. 'If that's what you want, sir. Young gentlemen like you don't stand a chance against trained professionals.' He raised his fists.

Mr Copperfield heard the thud of flesh on flesh and the next thing he saw was Bates laid out cold on the floor. Seeing their leader so easily defeated, the other two men both ran at Cain together. They wrestled him back against the wall.

'Oh I say! That's not fair!' objected Mr Copperfield. He looked round for a weapon to help Cain even the odds and lighted upon one of the legs of the camera stand. He struck one guard over the head with the metal pole. It bent in the middle and the man slumped to the ground.

'Good work, Mr Copperfield!' Cain delivered a left hook to the last man's jaw, putting him out of action. He shook his hand, knuckles feeling the impact. His gaze found Mr Wallace, who was standing open-mouthed on the far side of the room. 'You want to throw your hat in the ring too?'

The photographer shook his head.

'Then stay here and keep shtum. If I see you outside this room, I'll not be merciful.'

Cain strode out, Mr Copperfield hurrying to keep up.

'Shouldn't we go back for the boy?' Mr Copperfield asked, glancing nervously at the closed door to the room that held Burlington and Mel. It was too quiet in there. Guards waited outside, rifles at the ready.

'Viorica and the fairies are with Mel. She'll let us know if he needs us.'

'And how are we going to get the other prisoners free? I do not have the authority for that.'

'Then we find someone who does.' Cain jogged down the steps to the umbrella cupboard.

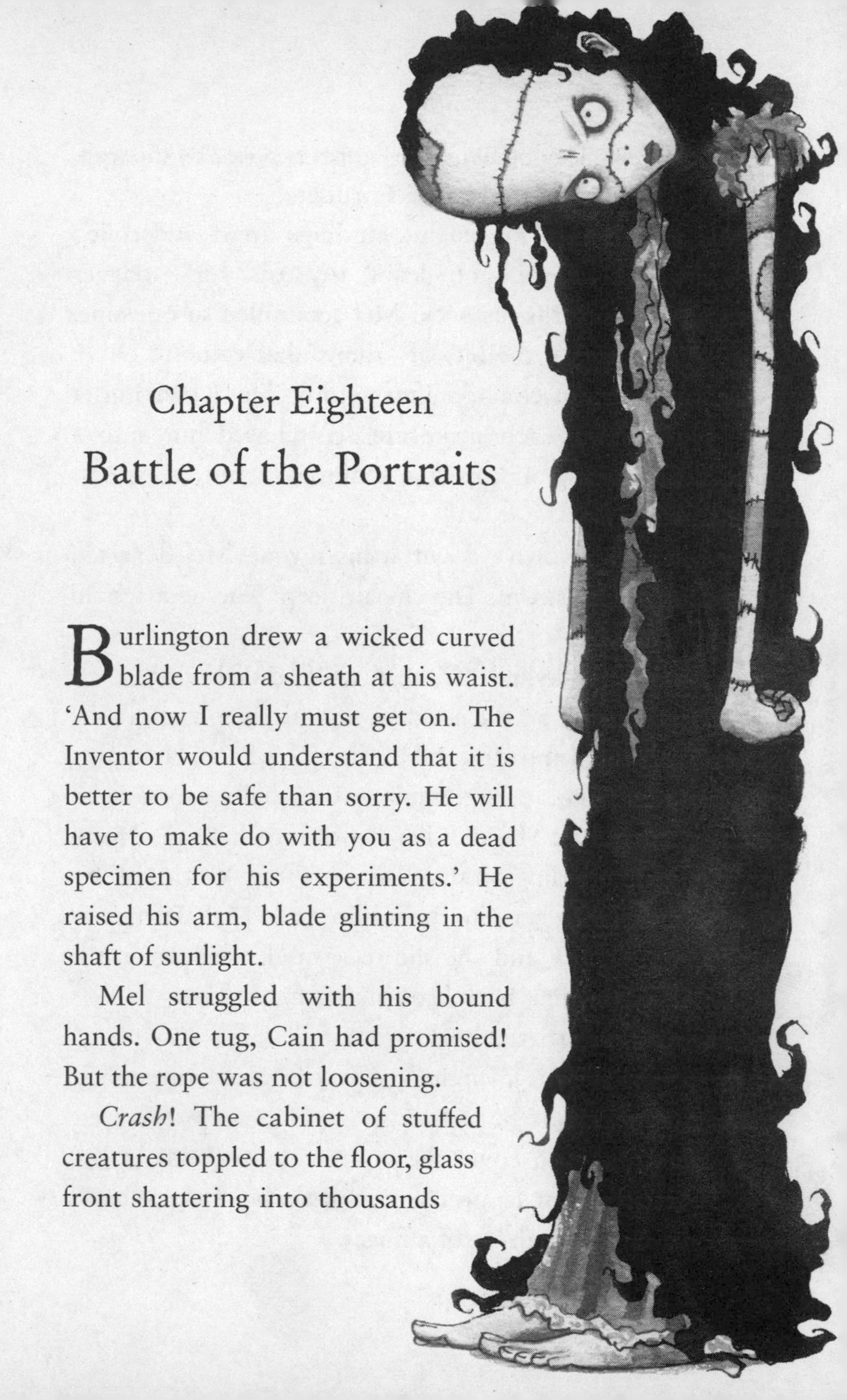

Chapter Eighteen
Battle of the Portraits

Burlington drew a wicked curved blade from a sheath at his waist. 'And now I really must get on. The Inventor would understand that it is better to be safe than sorry. He will have to make do with you as a dead specimen for his experiments.' He raised his arm, blade glinting in the shaft of sunlight.

Mel struggled with his bound hands. One tug, Cain had promised! But the rope was not loosening.

Crash! The cabinet of stuffed creatures toppled to the floor, glass front shattering into thousands of splinters, leaving two little figures exposed by the wall.

Burlington reared back. 'Intruders!'

At last, Mel tugged his bindings apart and rolled away, but Burlington leapt towards him, dagger slashing towards his neck. Mel scrambled to one side, throwing all of the bits of cabinet that came to hand: wood, broken china, a brass lamp. The Chief Butler grunted with each strike but still chased him into a corner, cutting off any chance of making it to the door.

'Got you!'

The blade drove down at his throat. Mel deflected it with his forearm. The cut bit deep. The next would kill him.

Then the skylight fell in. A wolf landed on the tiles. Viorica shook off the necklace of anti-pigeon spikes she had gathered and attacked Burlington's back. He swung round, slicing at the vampire wolf's belly as she went for his throat. She dug her claws into his sides, teeth snapping. Burlington shrieked and threw Viorica off his chest, heaving her into the wall next to Mel. There was a horrid *crack* and she slid to sprawl bleeding on the floor beside him, back broken, her fight over.

'Guards!' roared Burlington.

Monster Patrolmen charged into the room, rifles ready.

'Shoot them!' he ordered.

Mel tried to cover the wolf with his body, a last minute attempt to protect her. Rifle bolts drew back, ready for the squeeze of a finger.

'I said it was a stupid plan,' said Mel. 'Sorry, Viorica.' He squeezed his eyes shut, braced for pain.

'You will not hurt Mel Foster!' Eve jumped through the broken skylight and landed on six of the guards. The surviving riflemen shot wildly at her, bangs echoing around the room, holes appearing in the plaster.

A boy followed Eve, sliding sailor-fashion down a rope – Abel, now in the rough brother form. He fired a revolver at Burlington. The bullet hit but did not disable him. Like Eve, Burlington's flesh was obviously made of tougher stuff than an ordinary human.

The monster fairies launched themselves on the nearest Patrolman, biting his ankles and then his fingers as he swiped at them. Inky dragged his rifle from his grip and ran off with it, towing it out of the door. The man gave chase, shaking Nightie off his leg. Of the firing squad a single guard remained, as the others were all fighting Eve. Mel tackled him at the knees, bringing him down. They rolled over and over, both struggling to get control of the gun. Then Nightie leapt on to the man's back and dug his fingers up his nostrils. The man reared back, yelling, giving Mel the chance to bring the butt of the rifle up, muzzle pointed at the floor. The butt hit the man hard on the jaw and he collapsed.

'Thanks, Nightie,' said Mel, breathing heavily as he shoved the guard off him.

Looking round, Mel saw that Eve had made short work of the remaining Patrolmen. Abel was firing with cool determination, driving the Chief Butler away from Mel and towards the chair in the centre of the room. Abel's bullets didn't injure but acted like punches, throwing Burlington backwards with each hit.

Blind in her rage and heedless of her own danger, Eve saw that their arch-enemy was still on his feet. She charged at the Chief Butler.

'You!' she roared. 'You tried to kill Mel Foster!'

Grappling at the side of his chair, Burlington seized the harpoon and aimed it at Eve's chest. It had killed the biggest whale ever known, and Mel feared that even Eve's tough skin might not deter such a weapon at close range. With only a split second to think, Mel threw the pot of mummy oil on the ground in front of her. Eve's feet shot out from under her and the harpoon whizzed over her head. Slipping and sliding, she scrambled to her feet, still intent on crushing the butler. Seeing an enraged giantess heading for him, Burlington tugged a candle bracket on the wall. A hidden trapdoor opened at his feet and he jumped down into it. The top slid back behind him.

Eve ripped the entrance open with her bare hands but discovered that the passage below was too narrow for her. 'He is escaping! Coward!' Eve yelled after him.

'Enough, Eve, we can't risk going after him,' panted Mel.

She spun round and lifted him in a bone-crushing hug. 'You saved me!'

He tweaked her nose affectionately. 'That makes us about even, I guess.'

'Viorica!' Abel cried as he spotted his friend in the debris. He rushed to the wolf's side. Disentangling himself from Eve, Mel knelt beside the vampire, seeing no movement of her rib cage.

'I'm so sorry. I think she's dead. He threw her against the wall.'

'Of course she's dead. She's a vampire,' snapped Abel. He tapped the wolf's snout. 'Come on, transform! Now is not the time to have a fainting fit!'

No response came from the wolf, not even a twitch of a whisker.

'Smelling salts – I need smelling salts!' demanded Abel.

They were in the middle of a battlefield and Abel wanted something that usually could only be found in a lady's handbag!

Of course! 'Give me a moment!' Mel charged out of the room, Eve following. 'Lady Bracknell? Where's Lady Bracknell?' Not thinking, Mel grabbed the first person he saw walking dazedly about the foyer. Too late, he realized what he had done: it was the Dr Foster double. With a surprised exclamation, the portrait man puffed into non-existence.

'Oh no!' gasped Mel. It had always been the plan, but contemplation wasn't the same as actually doing the deed.

'Mel Foster, you are not to blame: you have carried

out your part. We wait for the raven. But first we help our friend.' Eve grabbed the next guard they came across. 'Where is the Lady Bracknell?'

Faced with her bared teeth, the man pointed shakily down the corridor. Eve let him go. 'Run away!' she bellowed at him. He sprinted for the exit.

The further reaches of the gallery were teeming with people: prisoners released from their cells battling Patrolmen trying to herd them back in. Cain had to have been at work here. The fighting intensified as they approached the largest of the exhibition halls. Mel and Eve found Lady Bracknell mustering her troops for a final stand against their foes. Blank canvases that had once held military scenes still hung on the walls while their occupants formed ranks before their new general. At Lady Bracknell's left side was Mr Squeers and on her right was Mr Gray, still looking impossibly elegant in the midst of battle. Facing them at the other end of the room were Cain and Mr Copperfield, along with the four people selected for the bonfire and numerous other prisoners and freed monsters. Two men dressed in scholarly gowns were in the process of changing into werewolves, snouts emerging from under mortar boards. Mel saw that things were not going his friends' way. They were being beaten back, afraid of injuring their own doubles and thus themselves. Added to that handicap, the painted troops did not stop for any injury.

'Mel!' shouted Cain. 'Can you blast them?

'I don't know!' shouted Mel. Could he risk it?

The raven swooped, croaking, 'Nevermore!'

What the blazes does that mean? wondered Mel desperately. 'Eve, what do I do?'

'My boy!' A sprightly older man in a dapper morning coat burst through the crowds behind him. 'What you *do* is send that lot back to their makers!' The revived Dr Foster started laying about him with his rolled umbrella, knocking Monster Patrolmen over like cricket stumps.

With a hoot of delight, Mel charged into the midst of the battle, exploding soldiers left and right. The air filled with a cloud of red, gold and brown paint flakes. Now the fortune of war was seesawing between the two sides. Mel saw the two Mrs Harkers grappling together, one with her hands around the other's neck. He rushed to her aid, touching where hand throttled throat. The fake exploded, releasing her gasping victim, who received a jolt of power that seemed to reinvigorate her.

'Hands off my Jonathan!' she shouted. Long blonde hair coming loose, she sprang back into the fray and laid out her husband's double with a nifty punch.

'Thank you, dearest. That was most . . . surprising.' Mr Harker brushed himself off. Mel quickly disposed of his double.

'Now I see where your strength came from, darling!' said Mr Harker, marvelling as energy zinged through his veins. Brimming with renewed life, the Harkers rejoined the battle, capturing Mr Squeers and bringing him cringing to his knees.

Since Mel had swung the day in their favour, Cain changed tactics: instead of fighting, he and his allies now herded the troops towards Mel, their ultimate weapon. A poltergeist threw picture frames at a fresh wave of Burlington's army, pinning a painted South Sea Islander to the ground so Mel could explode him. A hairy yeti with big feet stomped on a phalanx of hunting dogs from a Dutch landscape. Three vampire boys wrestled a Hercules to the ground, teeth snapping on canvas. There were only a few real people to deal with now: Mr Copperfield took out Dorian Gray with a bent camera pole and Eve scooped up a screeching Lady Bracknell. Mel rushed from group to group, sending the pictures back to their original elements of ink, oil paint, paper and canvas.

Last soldier turned back to dust, Mel wiped his eyes. Just one more. He touched the confused figure of the Queen in her state robes who had been wandering around the battlefield, waving at everyone. She puffed out of existence. There: that sorted out a potential constitutional crisis.

'This is an outrage!' screeched Lady Bracknell at Eve. 'I am a peeress. You cannot manhandle me like this!'

'Shut up!' Mel shouted at Lady Bracknell. Her cries were making it hard to think.

'You will be punished for this!'

'I said, shut up! Do you have any smelling salts?'

Of all the things he could have asked her, this was the last thing Lady Bracknell expected. 'What?'

'In a pocket, a handbag – anything.'

'A handbag?' she bellowed, outraged.

'Oh, never mind.' Seeing the bag caught in the crook of her arm, he wrestled it from her and shook it out. A little vial of smelling salts fell to the floor. He grabbed it. 'Thanks.'

Leaving Cain and Eve to secure their defeated foes, Mel raced back to Viorica in the semicircular room.

'What took you so long?' growled Abel.

Where to start? 'Here!' He thrust the bottle at Abel, who unstoppered its neck and waved it under Viorica's snout. He caught a whiff of it himself; the scent made his eyes water. The wolf's sensitive nose got the full blast. She shuddered and yelped.

'Transform, you daft creature!' Abel said tersely.

With a growl, the wolf turned to mist and reformed as a girl, long hair covering her body. Abel slipped out of his coat. 'Here, Lady Dracula.'

Mel and Abel turned their backs while the vampire dressed.

'Thank you,' Viorica said quietly, once she was decent.

Mel turned round, relieved to find her standing straight and unbroken. She looked fragile in the too-big-for-her coat. 'It's me who should be saying thank you,' he told her. 'I'd be dead if it weren't for you.'

She gave him a shy smile. 'Being dead isn't so bad, you know.'

'Where are the others?' Abel started loping towards the entrance hall. 'Ah, there you are, brother. I hope you have a good explanation for why you borrowed our shape in public?'

Cain grinned, flicking his auburn hair from his eyes. 'Don't worry: our friend Mr Copperfield has destroyed the evidence, and all witnesses will be gibbering wrecks by the end of the day. No one will believe them.'

'I do not gibber,' said Mr Copperfield stiffly.

'That you don't, sir,' replied Cain, slapping the elderly secretary on the back. 'I meant gibbering *hostile* witnesses. A good man in a tight corner is this one, Abel. I think we'll have to make him an honorary member of the Monster Resistance. You should have seen him wield that camera pole. Put him and Dr Foster together and I'd say we have a pretty unstoppable duo.'

Mr Copperfield and Dr Foster exchanged an embarrassed but proud look. 'Thank you. Most kind of you,' they muttered.

'Now, where has Burlington got to?' asked Cain, checking around him. 'His people are defeated but I do not see him. I was rather looking forward to the part where we have an abject butler in chains.'

'He's not just a butler,' said Mel. 'He told me he's been turned into an extra-strong human, a kind of super-man, by the Inventor's experiments.'

'He escaped into the sewers during the battle,' added Abel. 'He will have retreated to his lair, wherever that is.'

'His private quarters, Buckingham Palace,' said Mr Copperfield. 'He'll have gone back there.'

'Why?' asked Eve. 'He must know he is defeated.'

'Ah, mademoiselle, such villains are not so easy to put down,' said Cain. 'And we still haven't accounted for the Queen. Abel, do you know how to vanquish a super-being?'

Abel frowned. 'No. I thought that was your area.'

'Not mine. I'm certain we agreed you would look into it.'

'No, we did not. We discussed the theory, nothing more.'

It seemed the division of knowledge had failed them, but there was no time for a brotherly squabble.

The two fairies raced over to Mel and threw themselves at his ankles.

'You're alive!' Nightie squawked.

'I am – thanks to you and the others.'

'So, what now?' asked Inky, tiny fists clenched in preparation for the next battle.

'We take back control of the Palace and save the Queen,' said Cain.

'God save the Queen!' said Mr Copperfield, standing to attention.

'With a little help from us,' murmured Mel to the fairies.

Chapter Nineteen
The Widow's Spider

The Palace was suspiciously quiet when the Monster Resistance and their allies arrived in the forecourt. The skies had clouded over and in the distance a storm rumbled. Fat drops of rain splattered on the pavement. Glancing upwards, Mel saw the red standard with black pitchfork motif flapping in the stiffening breeze.

Cain handed out the whistles that he had taken from the Patrolmen captured at the National Gallery to Dr Foster, the Harkers and the other people and monsters who had come to support them.

'No need for you to come inside, Dr Foster,' Cain said firmly, 'but we'd appreciate it if you kept watch on all entrances and windows. Blow the whistle if you see Burlington – we don't want him slipping away. Make sure we can hear the signal. I think there's a storm coming.'

'There's a storm coming all right,' muttered Dr Foster. 'A storm of protest whipped up by an over-reaching butler.'

Under Dr Foster's command, Mr and Mrs Harker set about dividing up their forces with impressive efficiency, aided by the sound advice of Inspector Bucket. Mel got the impression that these three were all used to fighting unusual foes.

Cain knelt beside the two monster fairies who were looking eagerly at the Palace. 'Fairies, I am afraid I'm going to have to ask you to monitor the sewers for us.'

Inky's mouth fell open. 'Really?'

'Yes, I know it's going to require a complete set of new clothes and as many baths as you would like on return, but we need a warning if Burlington comes that way or tries to flee back into the maze of tunnels below our feet.'

Nightie gulped then saluted. 'Yes, sir.' He nudged Inky in the ribs.

'Yes, sir,' echoed Inky gloomily. 'We always get the rubbish jobs.'

'Good lads,' said Abel, heaving up a manhole cover. The fairies clambered inside. He gave each one a silver whistle, which perked them up a little. 'Stay out of sight if you meet him – just come to the surface and blow your whistle. Beware storm surges – these tunnels take the run-off from the roads.'

'Righto!' called Nightie, disappearing into the darkness.

Inside the Palace, the Monster Resistance found that the building was not deserted despite appearances. Lord Rosebery and the Prince of Wales were hiding in a side room where less important visitors were usually kept waiting; Moppet quivered at their feet, pink bow flopping down one side of her face. They emerged when they saw Mr Copperfield, though his unusual companions did give the gentlemen pause.

'Your Royal Highness, sir,' said Cain with aplomb. 'I don't suppose you have seen the Queen?'

The Prince of Wales shook his head, though his eyes kept going back to Eve. 'Young Jekyll, isn't it? Rum doings, boy, rum doings. I've not seen her for days. She won't see anyone but that awful butler person. I don't know what to do. This will be the end of the monarchy!'

'Let's not rush our fences, sir,' said Cain calmly. 'We are putting that to rights today. We just need to find her before her butler does.'

Mr Copperfield put up a hand. 'I have an idea that will save you a long search. Moppet, go find your mistress.'

The little dog quivered like a jelly.

'Please, be brave. She has biscuits.'

That did the trick. The dog bounded up the stairs. She did not stop at any of the ceremonial chambers but carried on climbing.

'Good gracious, I haven't been up here since I was a boy!' said the Prince of Wales, puffing away at the rear of the party. 'This is the nursery wing.'

'Silence from here on, please!' Cain waved them to stop. 'Just Resistance members to continue. Your Highness, Lord Rosebery, wait until we give you the all-clear. Mr Copperfield, look after them for us, please.'

Mel and the other Resistance fighters crept down a long corridor painted bright blue with a frieze of ducks at waist height – a bizarre place for a showdown with an arch villain. An old rocking horse stood against the wall, thick with dust. A snuffling came from one room. Easing the door open, Mel caught sight of a sad-looking pygmy hippo. No Queen.

Moppet carried on to the last room and scratched at the door.

'Who is it?' came a quavering voice from inside.

'Your Majesty?' Cain opened the door and they fanned out into the room. Mel stopped short near the entrance. The room was full of portrait doubles of the Queen's dead husband, Prince Albert. They sat or stood, reading newspapers, making their way through reports from the London Sanitary Committee, whittling a stick or chatting companionably together by the fireplace. They all ignored the old lady sitting in a rocking chair.

The Queen turned around, her eyes by some instinct going to Mel. 'Why does Albert not know me?' she asked. 'He thinks I am my grandmother. He doesn't recognize me,' she thumped her chest, '– me who has mourned him so faithfully, so long!'

Mel stood at her side, seeking the right words. 'They aren't really him, Your Majesty. These are just echoes.'

'I thought having him near would heal the pain, but in truth it makes it worse.' Her chin wobbled, her eyes filled with tears. 'I do not want to see him and not be known to him.'

'I can get rid of them, if you wish.'

She nodded. 'Do it.' She hid her face in Moppet's fur.

Mel went from prince to prince extinguishing the pretence of life. A light dust fell to the ground, leaving the widow alone once more.

'One has made a frightful hash of things,' the Queen said, dabbing her cheeks with a lace-edged handkerchief.

Mel opened his mouth to say something consoling when a dark shadow unfolded from the skylight in the ceiling. Like a spider on a thread, Burlington roped down on top of Mel, his boot threatening to crush his windpipe. Mel writhed and gasped but the pressure did not let up. The boots smelt of the sewers Burlington had had to crawl through.

Eve grabbed an empty cradle, meaning to heave it at the butler.

'Get back, all of you! One move and the boy dies.' Burlington cracked his whip and Viorica yelped as the end caught her leg.

Mel's friends froze, not daring to test the threat.

'Right!' Burlington scanned the room, taking stock of his opposition. The key gleamed on his bare chest and the leather of his trousers shone like a widow spider's thorax. Thunder rumbled overhead. 'Now I have your attention, here are my demands. I will take the boy and this old woman to Windsor and run the Empire from there. If I see any of you near us, the boy dies. If I hear of you again, the boy dies. You get the message?'

Eve put down the cradle and growled, fists flexing. Cain and Abel exchanged glances and nodded, holding their hands out to demonstrate that they were not armed.

Burlington heaved Mel up by the throat, his superhuman grip could crush the bones in his captive's neck at the slightest move of the Resistance. 'Come, Your Majesty, we're leaving.' He grabbed the old lady's elbow and dragged her along with them into the nursery corridor.

'Mummy!' shouted the Prince of Wales, rushing to aid her.

'Out of our way!' Burlington kicked the prince in the stomach. He fell backwards on to Lord Rosebery.

Burlington hurried Queen Victoria and Mel out into the garden at the rear of the Palace. Rain hammered the lawns and shrubbery, a heavy autumnal downpour that soaked them all to the skin within seconds. A manhole cover stood open in the courtyard.

'Down you go.' Burlington stood over the old lady,

water dripping from his jutting jaw and the ends of his dark hair.

'One does not go into sewers!' she cried, remembering her dignity.

'That's part of your kingdom too, Your Majesty. Get in – or do I have to push you? A queen with a broken leg is still useful to me.'

'Bertie!' the Queen called in distress.

The Prince of Wales limped out of the Palace, Cain and Abel supporting him on either side. 'Mummy, you had better do what he says for the moment. Fiend, don't you dare harm her!'

Burlington prodded her in the small of the back. 'Go on.'

Gathering her courage, the Queen felt for the ladder and began her slow climb down. Burlington kept his eyes on the Resistance, his grip tight on Mel's neck. Lightning flickered in the sky.

'I'll kill him if you follow.'

Eve looked ready to charge but Viorica held her back with a hand on her forearm.

'Do not,' she whispered.

'Mel Foster, I will come for you!' shouted Eve.

'Do that and he'll die.' Burlington checked that the Queen had reached the bottom of the ladder, then casually pushed Mel in after her.

Mel fell the eight feet to the bottom, landing with a splash in the water. He scrambled to his feet, boots sliding in the unspeakable slime, but before he could escape, Burlington had him in his grip again. He passed the Queen a lantern that hung on a peg fixed to the tunnel wall. 'Lead on, Your Majesty.'

The little old lady held up the light, her eyes shining with bitter determination. 'We will see you executed for this!'

Burlington smiled. 'The Inventor won't allow that. You will have to get used to taking orders from now on. Windsor is that way. Get going.'

'One cannot walk all the way to Windsor in the sewer!'

'No, but one can walk as far the getaway carriage that your humble butler has had the foresight to park in St James.'

'Humble? What tosh!' muttered the Queen, but she set off in the direction he had indicated.

Mel thought that he could hear scurrying ahead of them. The monster fairies would be tracking their movements, but he still needed a plan to get clear of Burlington. None of his friends would want to tackle the butler while he had his death grip on Mel's neck.

Then matters were taken out of his hands. Whistles sounded in the dark. The water rose suddenly from knees to waist.

'Storm surge!' Mel warned.

The Queen, both elderly and small, lost her footing. The lantern went out.

'Inky, Nightie: save the Queen!' Mel shouted.

'Where is she?' Burlington lunged forward, groping and splashing blindly in the water for the monarch. 'No!'

But nature had the tunnel in its more powerful grip. The water was building, now at chest height. Only Burlington's grasp on his neck stopped Mel being swept after the monarch.

'We've got to get out!' gasped Mel.

'Shut up! She has to be here somewhere!'

'If you don't go to the surface, we'll die.'

Those were the last words Mel managed to utter before the surge reached the ceiling. Mel felt his feet lifted from the ground. He took a breath and closed his eyes. The water carried him away.

Chapter Twenty
The Key

The only thing that kept Mel alive in the battering journey down the tunnel was the grip on his shoulder. Burlington refused to relinquish his one remaining hostage, so he dragged Mel to the surface with him when there was an air pocket allowing him to gulp a breath. Still the water pushed them onwards, drains from the paved streets shooting gallons of rain into the system as the storm continued to swirl overhead.

Finally Mel slammed against a vertical grating, water pouring past him. Burlington let go of him to tear apart the iron bars, and they both tumbled out into the River Thames below the outflow. Mel hit the water and went under, weighed down by boots and clothing. A hand seized his collar and hauled him up.

Burlington threw Mel on to the little shingle beach to one side of the drain exit. Rain streamed down, washing off the worst of the muck. Staggering to his feet, Mel looked up. The tower of Big Ben loomed over them. They had come out into the river by the Houses of Parliament.

Burlington punched the Embankment, leaving a crack in the stonework. 'We've lost the Queen!' He muttered dark curses.

Mel quickly scanned the shoreline, looking for a way off the mudbank. They were not far from the arch of Westminster Bridge. He remembered there being a boat landing stage just the other side – if he could get that far.

'It is no matter. I will simply rule in her stead,' announced Burlington, his voice cracking with desperation. He was clutching at straws, too stubborn to see he had lost. 'Come, boy, we will enter Parliament and take control from there. My Monster Patrolmen are still loyal to me.' With squelching strides, he bore down on Mel.

Mel broke into a run, heading for the steps beyond the bridge.

'No you don't!' Burlington tackled him from behind. Mel fell on to the gritty mud, all breath driven from his body by the huge weight that had landed on him. Thunder boomed across London.

'I'm not going with you!' shouted Mel, squirming to get free. 'I won't help you.'

Burlington pulled him up and shook him, like a

terrier with a sewer rat in his jaws. 'You'll do as I say.'

Mel swung a punch but only succeeded in grazing his knuckles on the key on Burlington's chest.

The Chief Butler laughed cruelly. 'Pathetic!'

Suddenly, a shaft of blinding light arced down from the clouds, accompanied by an almighty clap of thunder that deafened Mel. He felt a clean cold pain in every bone of his body. His world lit up like a Christmas tree, all reversed like a photographic plate. His scream joined with Burlington's bellow. The grip on his neck vanished and Mel found himself on his knees. Wiping his eyes, he saw Burlington lying on his back on the shore, the key smoking on his chest. It was glowing white hot.

Oh no, he's going to get the same power as me! Mel thought. He reached out to grab the key but, before he could touch it, Burlington curled up into a ball, screaming and hissing.

'No, no!' Burlington's voice was going higher, his body writhing and thrashing. His bronze skin paled; his muscles vanished. In one short minute, all the stolen life energy had drained back to the key.

Of course! The key had already been emptied of power when Mel had been lightning-struck as a baby. The same event now prompted it to recharge its strength from the nearest source: Burlington.

Mel snatched back his hand. He had no intention of losing his power as well.

Whistles on the bridge drew his attention upward.

People were gathering along the railings. There were shouts of 'I see them!' and 'There they are!'

'Mel Foster, I come for you!' bellowed Eve. Not bothering with the stairs, she jumped from the bridge into the shallow water near the shore. Making her way upstream, she hurried towards him.

'No, I won't go back to that life.' Burlington's voice was weedy and nasal and when he stood up, his thin chest was as puny as a plucked chicken, clothes hanging off him, hair flopping in his eyes. 'I won't let them take me!' He splashed off into the river, swimming out towards the main current. So used to his super-strength, his eyes rounded with alarm as the tide caught him.

'Help!' he wailed, swept under the arches of Westminster Bridge.

Eve stood with her hands on her hips. '*Sacre bleu!* Do not say I have to save him?'

Mel stumbled towards her. 'Please, Eve.'

Her eyes, one blue one brown, watched Burlington's head go under, then pop up again. 'And where do you want me to take him?'

Mel considered Burlington's last words. The Monster Patrolmen were still loyal to him, and he had the key round his neck. If he could work out how to reverse the draining process, he might still return to his old ways.

'When you reach him, please drop that key in the river, somewhere right in the middle where no one can dive to find it. But don't touch the key itself – just the chain – that thing's dangerous. Then I suggest you take him to Albert Docks and present him to Captain Mariner as the new cabin boy. Tell him the Queen will reward him well if he makes sure Burlington never leaves the ship again.'

'*Bon*. Now I go.' Sleek as a seal, Eve launched into the Thames and struck out for Burlington. Mel watched her scoop up the struggling butler in her arms and the pair vanished downstream. He doubted very much whether London would be seeing Burlington again.

As Mel turned for the stairs, he saw Cain and Abel waiting for him. Viorica stood a little behind them with a blanket.

'There you are, boy,' she said with her usual disdain. 'Keep down-wind: you smell horrible.' Despite her scorn, Mel was surprised to feel a little tender squeeze of his shoulder as she wrapped the blanket around him.

Cain touched him on the arm. 'All well, old bean?'

'Did you see what happened?'

'We came just as the lightning struck,' said Abel. 'We thought you were both goners.'

'So did I for a moment, but the key drained Burlington's strength. He went back to being his true self. I've asked Eve to make sure he never returns. It seems to me that he has too many supporters here to risk prison.'

'The key?' Abel's eyes glinted at the possibilities.

'Probably lost in the river by now. I didn't see it

round his neck after Eve rescued him.'

'Pity.'

'What about the Queen?' asked Mel, quickly changing the subject.

'Saved by Incubus and Nightmare,' said Cain, leading Mel through the curious crowds towards the carriage. 'They brought her up right outside the front door to Buckingham Palace. I believe the plan after that is a bath and a change of clothes before they are given their pick of the Queen's jewels as a reward.'

'They'll love that.'

'Do you want to join them? The Queen will wish to reward you for your part in bringing down Burlington.'

Mel shook his head, feeling all of the scrapes and bruises of the last few hours. 'Maybe later. Just now, I would like to go home.'

Burlington may have been banished, but there was still a lot of work to do clearing up his mess. London was still haunted by doubles, the old government had to be summoned to Downing Street, the guilty parties punished.

But not just now.

Now was a time for the Monster Resistance to gather in the Jekylls' library and take a well-earned rest. The mummy was waiting with a huge trolley bearing a pyramid of delicacies to celebrate their victory.

On seeing Mel come downstairs in fresh clothes,

the Egyptian shrugged in a 'what happened?' gesture. He had not seen anything after the revived Dr Foster jumped from the horseless carriage.

'It's good news, Mummy. We're home, the villain is exiled and the Queen is safe.'

The mummy lifted Mel off his feet and span him on the spot. Several of his bandages came undone and Mel had to spend five minutes doing him up again.

Eve squelched in from the street at that point and drenched everyone with Thames water as she shook herself off.

Mel, you are really all right?' she asked him anxiously, patting his arms to make sure.

'Never better, Eve.' He grinned.

Eve accepted a towel from Viorica and rubbed herself vigorously. The mummy poured a cup of tea for everyone and handed round buttered toast and sandwiches in the shape of sarcophagi. Jacob Marley hovered at his shoulder looking most upset that there was nothing to be upset about.

'Tell me the worst, sir,' he begged.

Mel let the others tell their tales. It was odd hearing his part from their points of view: they made him sound heroic whereas he felt that he had rather stumbled from one thing to the next, surviving on luck rather than judgement.

'It seems that Mel here has the magic touch, Marley,' said Cain, slathering jam on his toast. 'He can blast fakes with a full dose of life.'

Mel put his cup down. 'I am an experiment that went wrong, you might say.'

'Or Providence made sure it went right,' said Dr Foster. 'If this Inventor person is roaming the world doing terrible work, it is only right that his son is equipped to reverse his harm.'

Mel liked to think about it that way. They had defeated one enemy but the prime mover of the plot was still at large. The first battle had been won, but a war against the Inventor looked likely.

'How is Mr Copperfield?' Mel enquired.

'Instantly promoted to head of the Queen's household – a position that no one is calling Chief Butler, but we all know is the same thing. There will be a knighthood for him, I imagine,' said Abel, now taking his turn in the elegant brother form. He held his cup with smallest finger crooked.

'And what are they saying about the ex-Chief Butler?'

Cain laughed. 'I reckon they're already rewriting the history books about that. No one will want to admit they let a butler take over the British Empire.'

'They'll mock him and pretend he didn't matter,' added Abel. 'Laughter is the best way to damage an enemy.'

'Yeah, one silly song and your reputation is toast.' Cain bit into a piece and chewed with his mouth open.

'Have you given any thought to the future,

Melchizedek, now you are no longer on the Most Wanted list?' asked Dr Foster.

'I will look after him,' said Eve stoutly. The diamond-decked monster fairies sitting on her shoulders nodded vigorously.

'Of course, but he might also need a more . . . regular guardian. I would be honoured to adopt you, Melchizedek. You can come live with me and have a first class education – be a normal boy in a loving home.'

'Or,' said Cain, glancing at his brother, 'you could stay here, wear the Monster Resistance uniform, fight villains and pick up a few useful bits of information here and there. Absolutely no homework. Your choice.'

How far his life had come from his lonely days on board the *Albatross*, thought Mel. Looking round the circle of his friends – the sparklingly ugly fairies, the mummy and his cat, enigmatic Viorica, brilliant Cain and Abel, doleful Jacob Marley, the raven, and of course his best friend Eve – Mel knew what his answer would be.

'Thank you for your kind offer, Dr Foster, and I hope I can still come and see you regularly, but I think I'll stay here, if you don't mind. Who would be normal when they have the chance to be a monster?'

The MONSTER RESISTANCE WILL RETURN IN . . .

Mel Foster AND THE TIME MACHINE

FEARED STOLEN:

- the Crown Jewels,
- the Mona Lisa,
- the Czar's Fabergé egg collection

FOUND

one hunchback from medieval Paris, dumped on the streets of Victorian London

SUSPECTED

one ARCH VILLAIN with a TIME MACHINE

MEL FOSTER AND FRIENDS FACE THEIR MOST FIENDISH OPPONENT YET!